Stolen Heirs of Avaria

Michelle Mellor

Copyright © 2020 Michelle Mellor

All rights reserved.

ISBN: **9798651216796**

DEDICATION

To my parents who always believed in me

CONTENTS

1	Erika	1
2	Ida	4
3	Ida	7
4	Erika	12
5	Ida	17
6	Erika	22
7	Ida	26
8	Erika	30
9	Ida	37
10	Erika	42
11	Ida	48
12	Erika	54
13	Erika	59
14	Ida	66
15	Ida	73
16	Ida	78

1 ERIKA

Erika Fillmore hated waking up. Why live in reality with all of its hardships when you could dream of faraway lands, handsome princes, and daring adventures?

"Erika dear. It's time to wake up." Sang her mother through her shut door.

She slowly cracked her eyes open one at a time. "Do I have to?" She asked as she lay comfortably in her bed full of down.

"Yes dear, and do hurry it is your fifteenth birthday after all. I will send for your maid at once."

A loud groan escaped the room, "I shall get ready as fast as I can." The only assurance of her mother listening to her was the light footsteps moving away from her door after a few seconds of silence.

Erika slowly got out of her warm bed and stretched. She then walked across the cold wood floor to the wardrobe in the corner of the room. The door opened and her maid, Sarah, came into the room in a rush. Sarah hurried over to where Erika stood looking over her dresses.

"What dress will you wear today m'lady?"

Erika couldn't decide what to wear, so she said, "Surprise me." Sarah nodded nervously then began to go through the wardrobe. Erika walked over to her vanity and sat down. She studied her appearance carefully. Her long curly red hair was all knotted, her white skin made her look like a ghost. A ghost with freckles. You would never have guessed she was from England. A stranger would think she was from Scotland or Ireland, but Erika's father continued the line of English Barons in the family for the sixth generation. Erika was English all the way through.

She picked up the hairbrush and began to untangle her scarlet mane. When she had untangled only one side of her hair, from behind her Sarah held up a simple lavender day dress. "Would this dress suit you m'lady?"

Erika turned and nodded. She then stood and walked over to her screen and hid behind it as she changed while Sarah handed her the dress. When she was dressed Erika continued to brush her hair. Sarah had offered to do it for her, but Erika liked untangling her own hair. The process calmed her, and usually hurt less.

Finally, she was presentable enough to go to breakfast. She went down the stairs into a large and lavish living room that housed all kinds of expensive paintings and vases. Erika went down a hallway filled with paintings of her ancestors. There was almost every single Fillmore that had ever lived in her home in London. The hall finally ended along with the line of paintings.

Erika stopped at the huge double doors that led to the dining chamber. She took a deep breath, and then slowly opened the doors, "Happy Birthday!" Her whole family shouted. The room was filled with the interesting smell of kipper and eggs, her favorite breakfast meal. She quickly sat down now famished after smelling the mouthwatering food. She sat between her sister, seventeen year old Ida, and her grandmother.

Erika had always secretly harbored some small feelings of jealousy towards her sister. Ida had long chocolate hair. And her eyes were brown and green contrasting to Erika's electric blue ones.

Erika hurriedly ate her breakfast as she thought of what the day would bring. Would her father take her riding? Or would her mother take her to the dressmakers? But, whatever happened, she was sure the day was to be perfect.

"Erika, Erika!" Her brother Thomas pulled her back to reality. "Erika it's time for you to open your presents." Erika noticed everyone had finished eating as her father motioned to their butler Charles Goodwin. Charles then left the room and promptly came back struggling to carry more than a dozen beautifully wrapped presents.

Erika took one last bite of her eggs then along with her family, moved to the drawing room. She took a seat in the middle of the room where all her family members could see her.

She picked up a pretty light pink box from the pile of presents Charles had set beside her. She read the name tag. The present was from Ida. She carefully untied the yellow ribbon then opened the box.

Inside was a beautiful emerald green silk dress with lighter green ivy embroidery along the hem and neckline. She thanked her older sister then proceeded to open another gift. This present was a sea foam green box with a light pink ribbon.

She delicately opened the box. Inside was her grandmother's favorite silver heart locket. She looked at her grandmother in shock, "Oh grandmother, I cannot accept this, it's your most prized possession!" Her grandmother shook her head, "You keep it now, and it is in your hands from this point on." Uncertain, Erika slowly clasped the locket around her neck.

"Erika!" Her twin brothers Will and Thomas exclaimed, "Look behind-" Her brother Will was cut off by a guard running into the room.

Erika frowned until she saw the silver dagger sticking out of the guard's neck. She screamed in horror.

The guard gasped out one word "Run." Then he dropped to the floor and breathed his last breath. A puddle of blood surrounded him staining the floor permanently.

Everyone stood perfectly still in fear. Then, an arrow spun into Charles's back with a wet thwack. Men's roars echoed throughout the house. Erika's family stood up and huddled in a circle. Her father drew his sword. Two other guards ran into the room with their weapons drawn and stepped in front of the family.

Men so bedraggled it looked as if they had walked across all of England and Ireland to get to their home entered the room. The men came at them ferociously, swords in hand. One man, obviously the leader, stalked towards them. He was a giant of a man with a hulking ox-like body, and a shiny bald head.

He made a forward gesture to his men and the brutes surrounded the family. Erika could barely hear the big man say to his men, "Only take the Princesses." Her mind raced trying to figure out what he could have meant only when she looked up did she see a sword hilt coming towards her head. Before she could contemplate what was happening, the hilt reached its target.

Sharp pain spread throughout her head. She fought to stay awake. The last thing she heard before she lost consciousness was Ida's ear splitting scream.

2 IDA

Ida woke up with a pounding headache. The throbbing in her head made her vision go fuzzy. Slowly the pain subsided and she began to be able to see clearly.

Once her vision cleared she could see her surroundings. She was in a little room with no windows or furniture and one of the walls curved. The only exit she could see was a big oak door on the far side of the room

She panicked. Where was she? Why was she there? Then, it all came rushing back to her. She remembered the barbarians coming to her house and their guard and their butler Charles on the drawing room floor dead.

Ida began to cry. Charles had always been kind to her and she hated to think that he was gone along with the guard that had tried to warn her family of the danger behind him.

Suddenly, the large door opened revealing the big bald man she had seen before she had lost consciousness. "Follow me." The man said in a low scratchy voice, then simply turned around and walked down a hallway. She thought of her other option, refusing to go with him. But she gave in and walked down the hall towards the man curious of what she would find beyond the small space of the hallway. The hallway ended at a stairwell. The stairs looked as if they had once been burned.

They climbed the creaky charred stairs into a black starry night. Ida looked around hoping to see land but only saw the dark expanse of the ocean. She panicked suddenly even more scared than she already was.

"Come." She had not realized that the man had been waiting for her to follow him. She quickly followed hoping no one would hurt her. They went up a set of stairs. The man stopped at a door she guessed was to the Captain's quarters.

The mahogany door had a skull with two criss crossed arrows engraved into it. She gasped as she realized she was on the ship of the feared Captain William Hilyard.

The gruff man knocked on the door. "Come in." Came from within the chamber. The big man motioned for her to go in. Reluctantly she opened the door and entered the room too afraid of what would happen if she did not.

The first thing that entered her mind when she went into the room was "dark." The room had a big window in the back but it was covered with a silver curtain. Her eyes adjusted then she saw her.

Her sister Erika was lying on a small couch unconscious. She ran to her concerned. "Erika, please wake up." She shook her gently. Erika groaned and opened her eyes slowly.

"Where are we?" Erika asked after she stretched and rubbed her eyes.

"You girls are on the magnificent ship the Siren's Chanty of course." The girls turned towards the voice terrified. Standing in the shadows was a thin man. The man's eyes were swamp brown, his hair greasy and as black as night. He could have been handsome at one time but his appearance had been worn down by time and the stress of reality. The man looked familiar but she couldn't quite remember if, or where, she had seen him before. He walked over to the red mahogany desk and sat down. The desk housed some papers that looked so old they could have been around when Julius Caesar was born. "I am truly sorry for the inconvenience of your stay."

Ida was furious. "You would not have to apologize if you would not have kidnapped us in the first place!" The man stared at her for a few minutes then suddenly started to laugh. His laughter was so grating Ida almost found herself covering her ears. "This is not funny." She insisted appalled at his response.

He calmed down then said, "Aye, you are right, this isn't funny, you just remind me of someone. But since I brought you here I might as well tell you girls why. You see, I was once a very powerful person. But that soon changed, I lost everything I had. I lost my power, my wealth, even my true love, my amour. After losing everything I had ever worked for I ran to freedom. I ran to the sea. Now, my revenge is near. I will destroy the very people that destroyed me. I'm building an army that will leave nothing in its wake."

The girls were confused, terrified, and furious. "Why would we help you?" Asked Ida. The Captain sat back in his chair and folded his arms.

"Do you not want to see your family again? If you help me I will see to it that they are returned to you after you do what I want you to do."

Suddenly a knock sounded on the door.

"Come in." The Captain barked. A young man about twenty years of age, three years older than Ida, came into the room Erika panicked although she was luckier than Ida who did faint dead away from fear. She glanced at the sharp double sided axe the man held in his hand.

"Captain, this is a gift to you from a merchant. He said to tell you he wished your amour a good evening." Erika sensed the faint fear in his voice. The Captain's gaze turned to the axe, and stared at it in contemplation for a moment before he remembered that there were people watching him. "Peter, show these girls to their chamber."

Erika's eyes widened in alarm, "Wait! You still haven't told us what has happened to our family and why we are here." Ignoring Erika, Peter, the man that had presented the Captain the axe, put the weapon down on the desk then turned to the girls, his eyes passing over Ida's face in interest.

He picked her unconscious sister up as if she was a doll. Then he easily dragged Erika outside onto the ship's deck.

"Do you have a death wish? Don't ever talk to the Captain like that again or he will kill you and your sister no matter how valuable you are to him. The only thing keeping you alive is by not knowing what is going on. Don't ask any more questions if you wish to live."

Erika nodded then followed him to her room.

3 IDA

Ida was horrified that she had fainted when Erika might have needed her. She awoke in a hammock swaying with the slightly tipping boat.

"Look who's finally awake." She looked to her right and saw Erika smiling down at her.

"How long have I been asleep?"

"Oh, about ten minutes or so." Ida noticed the clothes draped over her sister's arm.

"Are those for me?" Erika nodded and handed them to her. She then pointed her towards a curtain draped in a corner of the room. She then went inside the dressing room. Ida was instantly embarrassed of her new clothes. She had been given a blood red skirt that dropped scandalously to her shins, an all-black blouse, and black leather boots that went all the way up to her knees.

When she stepped out from behind the curtain, for the first time Ida realized Erika also wore the new scandalous clothes too. Her sister now wore a dark blue skirt, an all-white blouse, and brown leather boots that also went to her knees.

"Erika, what happened after I um, fainted?"

Erika smiled at her coyly, "After you fainted the young man, Peter, gave the terrifying double-bladed axe to the Captain," Ida frowned when her sister mentioned the Captain. Erika continued, "The man said the axe was a gift from a merchant who said to tell the Captain he wished his amour a good evening. The Captain then sent us away. I tried to ask him questions but they forced me out of the room. After exiting the room Peter told me not to ask any more questions or else we would be killed." Ida began to cry and Erika soon joined her and the two girls sat and hugged each other.

"Erika, do you think we'll ever see our parents ever again?" Ida wiped at her eyes with the hem of her old dress.

"I hope so."

The girls surveyed the small cabin they had been given for the time being. Suddenly the ship heaved onto its starboard side. The pair shrieked in surprise as they fell, sliding into the wall of the cabin. A few seconds after hitting the wall the door swung open revealing the young man, Peter, from before.

"Come, hurry." They scrambled to their feet and climbed towards the door. On the deck was a massacre. Another ship called the Cursed Serpent had placed itself beside the Siren's Chanty.

Smoke drifted throughout the air burning Ida's lungs. An arm pulled her back just as a cannon ball flew past the spot she had just been. She heard a voice that sounded far away then Erika was pulling her towards the stars that led to the Captain's quarters.

They ran up the stairs and entered the cabin. The two huddled together under the big mahogany desk hoping to be safe. They listened to the clang of swords and the sickening screams of dying men.

Then, the door creaked open. Footsteps creeped closer until the person was standing directly in front of the girls. Ida looked up to see the person had the Spanish royal coat of arms embroidered on his shirt sleeve, a privateer. Erika put her hand over Ida's mouth so she would not scream.

The privateer went through the different papers on the desk until he finally found what he was looking for. He tucked an old paper into his boot then turned to leave. The door then opened and closed one last time. The girls sat there silent, not daring to move.

When the battle was finally over, the person who found the girls was the Captain's first mate Rotten John. Rotten John led them outside to the deck. The air smelled strongly of gunpowder and blood. The crew was already swabbing the deck, helping the wounded, throwing the dead into the sea, and taking the sail down to repair.

The Captain walked over to the girls his face filled with

fear. "Where have you girls been?"

Ida took a deep breath then said shakily, "We hid in your quarters until the privateer came in and took one of the papers on your desk." The Captain's face turned as pale as a ghost's. He turned around and hurried into his quarters and Erika, Ida, and Rotten John rushed after him. They got to the room as the Captain was hastily going through all of the papers on his desk. He kept muttering over and over where is it? Where is it?

"Sir, what are you looking for?" Rotten John inquired. The Captain looked up at everyone.

"The key to my survival in this war." The room went silent. Ida was as confused as she was scared.

"Could you please elaborate?" She managed to say without her voice quivering.

The Captain sighed. "The map contained the location of three mythical artifacts with various powers that I could use to win the war. I would have my own secret weapons."

"But what are these artifacts exactly, and war against whom?" Ida asked. The cabin was silent for a minute as everyone awaited an answer.

"A feather from a phoenix that has the power to heal any wound or disease. King Arthur's sword Excalibur that can show the user the future. Lastly, Mjolnir the Norse god Thor's hammer that can produce and throw lightning." Everyone was quiet when he finished, not sure of what to say.

"And why do you trust us, your prisoners, with this information?" Said Ida.

"I am giving you this information because you are a part of my plan to reclaim these items." He paused, "And if you tell anyone my plans I will kill your family."

Rotten John muttered under his breath, "These artifacts are myths, they are not real." The Captain walked to the door.

Before he left he said, "As a pirate I have learned one thing, all myths are real."

Rotten John grimaced at his comment being heard by the Captain.

Peter then escorted the girls back to their cabin. In their cabin, Ida sat deep in thought. She thought about her family and when she would get to see them again. Then, her thoughts shifted to the Captain's plan to get the three artifacts before she finally drifted off to sleep.

    Over the course of the next week Ida and Erika were given supervised lessons in weaponry, a gift from the Captain, or so he said. Ida thought the lessons were the Captain's way of showing his superiority. As the week went by the Captain began to give the girls more freedom, but Ida and Erika never once trusted him. They did everything they were told, but only to survive and not suffer the Captain's wrath.

    One night the Captain told the crew they were going after the map. Everyone had agreed to go along with the plan. The next night Ida sat on her bed sharpening the knives she now wore around her waist at all times. All of a sudden the door opened to reveal Erika in the doorway.

    "The privateer's ship is within sight we will soon be within fighting range, you should get ready." Ida nodded and her sister left the room. She sheathed her knife carefully. The Captain had warned the girls that if they tried to hurt any of his crew intentionally or not, they wouldn't live to see the next day. Ida had been taught knife throwing, Erika had been taught archery. But they had both agreed to never use their weapons to kill a person intentionally.

    Ida buckled her belt around her waist then followed Erika above deck. The Cursed Serpent was only about two miles away. The Captain was at the helm steering the ship due north. The ship's thirty-four cannons were loaded, ready for combat.

    "Captain." A man yelled, "They've seen us." The Cursed Serpent was now turning around to face them. Ida took her position on the foremast just as ropes were hooked by each crew onto the other ship. The men then proceeded to fight each other to the death.

    The smell of blood and smoke in the air was nauseating. Ida stared down at the struggle trying to hide from view. Erika on the mainmast also stayed out of sight.

    But four men saw and pointed at Ida then started to climb the ropes that led to the crow's nest of the foremast.

    She aimed for the first man and waited. She panicked as she looked down after a short moment. The four men were so close to her she could see the few black crooked teeth that remained in their mouths.

Ida tried to frantically get Erika's attention. She waved her arms hoping her sister would see her. Just as the first man was a foot away from Ida, an arrow thumped into his back. Blood splattered Ida's blouse and skirt.

Another arrow whizzed pass her face missing the next man and hitting the crimson sail.

Suddenly she came out of her stupor, grabbed a knife and stabbed the next man in the arm causing him to fall taking the other men with him.

Ida looked to Erika who had tears dripping down her face. They both stared down at the fighting in shock of what they had just done.

The rest of the battle was a blur, Ida, and Erika, watched from above as the crewmen of both ships fought each other, and stayed out of sight of all pirates.

When there was only the privateer left, the girls came down from their spots in the foremast and mainmast. They crossed onto the privateer's ship along with the rest of the crew. The Captain was leading the privateer to the helm of the ship. He strapped the man to it with a rope as thick as Rotten John's bicep.

"Since you stole from me you deserve a much worse punishment, but this will have to do." The Captain fingered something in his pocket, "Everyone to the boat." Suddenly everyone ran to the ropes to be the first off the enemy boat. When everyone was safely off the cursed vessel the Captain bellowed at Erika as he gestured towards a torch, "Would you do the honors my dear?"

Fearing for what would happen if she didn't do what the Captain asked of her Erika nodded slowly, her face filled with dread. She sluggishly lit an arrow on fire, aimed, and then let the arrow fly. It hit the middle of the white sails. Flames raced across the sail and down the mast onto the rest of the ship. Ida watched the ship and the ship's crew burn as the Captain's crew made ready to sail. As they sailed away Ida couldn't take her eyes away from the pillar of smoke in the distance.

The Captain was truly a person to fear.

4 ERIKA

Erika looked to the east to see a faint mushroom cloud of smoke drift up into the sky. The memory of killing that man flashed into her mind. She hadn't meant for the arrow to pierce the man's back, she was trying to give him a warning to back off.

And when the Captain had asked her if she would light the privateer's boat on fire, she had said yes so he would not release his ire on Ida or herself.

"Erika." A voice sounded behind her. She turned so she was face to face with Rotten John, the Captain's emotionless henchman. "The Captain wants you in his quarters." Erika nodded in reply. She took one last glimpse of the fading smoke then slowly walked away. Ida, Peter, and Rotten John were already in the Captain's quarters.

"Now, that we are all here, I can tell you exactly what my plans are for the future," The Captain grinned his unnerving grin. He spread a map onto the table with his large beefy hands. Erika could barely read the small script. "This is the first item we need to find and obtain." He pointed to a place on the map. Erika gasped. By an almost invisible golden feather the map read London, England.

Peter backed away from the massive desk as fast as he could. "I… I know where it is." He managed to stutter.

The Captain's face lit up in excitement and another emotion Erika couldn't name, "Where my boy. Where is the treasure?" Erika saw Peter visibly swallow.

"My mother has it." At this point everyone was puzzled.

"Why would your mother have a phoenix feather in her possession?" The Captain stroked his beard in curiosity.

Peter cleared his throat clearly uncomfortable, "My mother is, Margaret Radforth, Queen of England."

Everyone gasped in shock except for Rotten John whose face was fixed in a permanent scowl.

The Captain's face slowly drew into a wicked smile, "I have a proposal." He rolled the map up then carefully put it into the desk drawer. He had the attention of everyone in the room. "I propose you three go and acquire the feather for me." He looked directly at Erika, Ida, and Peter.

Suddenly enraged, Erika clenched her fists and her face slowly turned red, "Why would you think we would help you steal after you kidnapped us!" Ida put her hand on her sister's arm as to warn her to stop talking, "We already lost our family, you can't force us to help you, we have nothing more to lose."

The Captain looked at Erika almost sorrowful, "I think you'll find that you have so much more to lose than you know." Erika's anger melted into fear as the Captain unsheathed his cutlass and pointed it at Ida. "You should think before you speak." Erika nodded submissively. "Now," The Captain began, "You three will do exactly as I say. Tomorrow morning we shall arrive at Aldeburgh, England. From there you shall travel by coach to London and shall stop only to switch coaches halfway through your journey. In London you shall win the queen's favor then steal the feather. I shall then come to you once you have triumphed." He locked the drawer he had put the map in, "Leave me, you shall need to prepare for your journey."

The next morning they laid anchor at Aldeburgh, England. The sunrise turned the sky a mix of scarlet, yellow, and indigo. Erika gazed at the beautiful sight wishing she could share the vision with her family.

She looked away. Ida and Peter were consulting the Captain about the plan. Erika finally walked over to them. At the same moment, the Captain looked at his pocket watch and told everyone it was time to start their journey.

The trio along with the Captain and Rotten John walked off the boat and across the wooden sun bleached dock to the town square. The only thing Erika heard was the eerie silence of a deserted town. "Where is everyone?" She asked.

Out of the corner of her eye she spotted a shadow moving toward her and she turned around as fast as she could. Behind her was a strange lady with fair, snowy hair. The sword the lady wielded was raised above her head.

Erika screamed and everyone looked turned to see the lady, the Captain's face grew pale.

"Run." He grunted to the girls. They didn't hesitate and scrambled to the nearest building.

Erika turned the doorknob hard but it wouldn't budge. She glanced behind her to see the Captain, Peter, and Rotten John immersed in battle with the lady.

They sprinted to the next building hoping the door would open. The door opened easily and they quickly went inside the building.

Inside the shop were a few dresses in all different sizes. The girls ran to the back of the room and hid behind a rack draped with violet fabric. The only sound in the building was the girl's labored breathing.

All of a sudden the door opened and the hinges squeaked. Erika looked around the fabric then hurriedly hid again. Standing in the doorway was the fair haired woman.

The woman slowly began to walk through the aisles of dresses and fabric. She stopped in front of the violet fabric, "Erika, Ida, you must come with me. You don't understand how dire this situation is. I'm your..." She said but the girls didn't hear the last word.

Erika turned to Ida. "Follow my lead." She whispered. Her sister's face went from scared to terrified. Erika suddenly pushed the rack they had been hiding behind onto the woman.

The two ran out of the building and locked the door so the eerie woman wouldn't be able to get out for a time.

In the median of the town square laid the Captain unconscious. The girls hurried to stand beside him. "Could we escape now?" Erika asked Ida. Her sister shifted on her feet uncomfortably. "It might be our only chance." The girls began to step away from where the Captain lay.

"What has happened to the Captain?" Said a voice to the

right of the girls. They turned to see Peter running towards them.

"He has been injured." Said Erika as she quickly stepped towards the Captain's limp body. Peter crouched down next to the Captain.

"I think he was only hit in the head. Where is Rotten John?"

Erika and Ida looked around the deserted town. "We'll go find him." Said Erika. They ran from shop to shop trying to find Rotten John. Finally they found him gagged with his hands and legs tied up in a bakery. Erika untied him then pulled the rag out of his mouth.

"Is the Captain injured?"

The girls nodded. Rotten John muttered something under his breath then hurried outside. The girls followed slowly. They had lost their chance of escaping. There was no hope for them now.

The Captain was now awake. He stood up with help from Peter and Rotten John. "You three must leave now!" They all nodded in agreement. They found the coach the Captain had paid to drive them to Witham, where they would then change coaches. Inside the coach, Erika decided it was the most cramped space she had ever been in.

On their way to Witham the three quickly warmed up to each other. They told stories of their past and sang songs. Erika and Peter warmed up to each other but Ida had always been quiet, and had never felt comfortable enough to talk to strangers, or men.

It had been fortunate that Peter had accidentally left his tin whistle in his pocket.

"You should sing." Erika said to Ida. Her sister quickly shook her head.

"No, I really shouldn't."

Peter looked at Ida curiously.

"Oh come on. I'll sing with you." Erika sat in silence for a few aggravating seconds. Ida needed to come out of her shell or she would never survive in the world.

Her sister finally nodded, "Okay, but only one song."

"Fantastic." Said Erika, "Why don't we sing The Pirates Life Of Old." Peter licked his lips then began to play a jaunty tune, and then the two sung the song as a duet.

The pirate life of old was none but gold and now it's filled with magic
Heave Ho the pirate life was filled with danger and magic
Heave Ho the pirate life was filled with death and gold
The waves were full of graves but no one gave until the final breath
Heave Ho the pirate life was filled with danger and magic
Heave Ho the pirate life was filled with death and gold

After finishing the song the trio stayed silent as their attention drifted to their thoughts. When all of them were exhausted the coach finally rolled into Witham.

The inn they decided to stay at was called the Lattice Inn. The innkeeper was a plump man with frizzy gray hair and spectacles.

"Good sir, we are wondering if you might have two rooms for us to stay the night." Peter said nervously.

"I only have one room left, " Peter nodded slowly.

"One room will be fine thank you." He handed the man the necessary payment. As the innkeeper walked away Peter said to the girls, "You two get some rest and I will watch out for Victoria outside." Victoria must have been the blonde woman at Aldeburgh. Erika and Ida nodded in agreement with his plan.

That night the girls laid in a bed as hard as a rock while Peter fought against the sleep that eventually overtook him.

At dawn the trio hurriedly ate their morning meal then set off on their adventure.

5 IDA

Ida sighed in relief when she finally stepped out of the stuffy coach onto the crowded streets of England's capital city London. Shops lined the streets. Merchants shouted prices of their exotic goods. The air was filled with the aroma of pies, cakes, spices, and different kinds of fruit.

She looked at all the shops longing for the streets of her home, suddenly overcome with homesickness for the security of Lowestoft, England. She held back the tears that suddenly overwhelmed her.

All of a sudden Ida was swiftly thrown back into reality as people started to scream and holler as a behemoth carriage twisted through the narrow lane. Everyone ran trying to find shelter within the chaos.

Peter pushed Erika and Ida inside a shop filled with the smell of pungent perfume.

Ida waited throughout the few seconds of turmoil holding her breath until the sound of screeching axles faded into the distance.

Finally, Peter said under his breath, "The carriage is gone, we are safe."

The trio exited the shop and started to slowly make their way to the palace where the crown prince would finally return home.

Upon arriving at the magnificent door of the palace Peter knocked on it soundly. Two guards opened the door revealing an old plump man with a thin, curled, moustache that Ida could only assume was the butler.

The man's kind brown eyes widened to twice their size when they passed over Peter. "My goodness." He whispered quietly. "Peter?"

Peter grinned like a madman. He probably was one; he had joined the Captain's crew after all. "Edwin, I thought I would never see you again. It has been too long. Girls!" Peter started enthusiastically, "This is my family's butler Edwin Debois."

Edwin led them inside after they had all been introduced. He led them through a grand hallway and into a large magnificent throne room. A blood red carpet led to the two elegant thrones made of beautifully carved wood. In the middle of the room was a colossal crystal chandelier. Tapestries portraying legendary battles, beautiful gardens, and endearing landscapes lined the stone wall.

All of a sudden a man and woman entered the room from a door behind the thrones. The couple sat on the thrones then the woman spoke, "One year. It has been a whole year since we last saw you. Peter Henry Radforth what do you have to say for yourself?"

Before Peter could answer his parents stood up and rushed to hug him. After a moment his mother, the Queen, said to him, "Now answer my question."

Her vibrant green eyes bore into Peter uncomfortably and he squirmed slightly, "I have been." he paused for a moment as if deciding how much of his story to tell his parents, "I have been sailing as first mate to a privateer."

Ida noticed he had lied directly to his parents. Queen Margaret Radforth's face turned as red as her dark hair. The man standing next to her was Peter's father, King William Radforth. The king was a tall broad man with a black beard and hair streaked with gray. It was said he had been very handsome in his youth.

The king turned to his wife, "Darling, it doesn't matter what Peter has been doing away from home. He's here now so we should look to the future instead of the past. But I do want to know who these young ladies are."

Peter cleared his throat harshly, "Mother, father, may I present the lady, uh, Eleanor Smith," He motioned to Erika, "and the lady, Diana Smith. They are the daughters of the Duke of Havershire." He then motioned towards Ida who immediately flushed.

Ida was alarmed at Peter's imaginary story. She didn't know how to act like a Duke's daughter; she was only a daughter of a Baron after all.

The queen looked confused, "May I inquire as to why they are here?" Unexpectedly her face lit up. "Oh, they must be here for the ball. Although, it is a little early to arrive."

Erika carried on the conversation, "Yes, your majesty, we are indeed here for the ball. But sadly while traveling we were robbed of all our luggage by highwaymen. We no longer carry our invitations or our gowns."

The queen's face twisted in sympathy, "You poor dears. I will personally have my seamstress sew you new dresses. And I will see to it that both of you have a room in the palace to stay in until the ball." She looked thoughtful for a moment. "Annarealia!" The queen called.

A strikingly beautiful young woman waltzed into the room. The woman who must have been Annarealia clearly looked exactly like Peter. They had the same golden hair and emerald green eyes sparkling with mischief.

I almost forgot that Peter had a twin sister. Ida thought. Everyone in England knew of the royal twins.

"Annarealia." Said the queen as the woman ran to Peter and hugged him. "Would you please show our guests to their rooms?"

"Of course mother." Annarealia motioned to Erika and Ida and reluctantly left Peter. "Come."

After Erika was settled into her room, Annarealia showed Ida her own room. A silver rug covered the oak flooring. A plush ornate bed lay in the middle of the room.

Ida sighed at such comfortable living conditions.

"I hope everything is to your satisfaction." Annarealia said.

Ida glanced at the woman, "Oh, yes, it is wonderful. Thank you for all of your help."

Annarealia turned to leave then suddenly exclaimed, "I almost forgot, I was going to lend you a few of my dresses until we can get a seamstress to make you some new ones including a ball gown."

Ida was shocked at such kindness and tears began to form in her eyes, "Thank you, your highness that would be most kind of you, but you do not need to share your dresses."

Annarealia wrinkled her nose in distaste, "Please, call me Anna, and I would be delighted to lend you my dresses, I only ask for one thing in return." Ida looked at her quizzically. Annarealia, or Anna, thought for a moment then smiled, "I only ask you to be my friend. You see, it gets torturously lonely here being the only person my age, and you are around my age are you not?"

Ida nodded and smiled, "I will gladly be your friend."

Anna smiled, "Then, let us go to my chambers to find a few dresses that fit you shall we." The two girls made their way towards Anna's chambers.

Anna's wardrobe was filled to the brim with beautiful day dresses, nightgowns, and ball gowns. Ida carefully looked through the glamorous dresses until she found a scarlet day dress with fashionable sleeves that went down to the elbow then flared. The neckline was higher than the latest style and was trimmed with white lace.

She also picked royal blue, yellow, and lavender dresses.

Anna sighed and said, "They will look perfect on you!"

After Ida had decided which dress she would wear she hurried to her room to prepare for dinner. Ida was looking at herself in the mirror thinking about how to make herself appear presentable when the door opened.

When she turned around, standing by the door was a maid that was around her mother's age. The maid moved towards Ida with a motherly smile, "M'lady, Princess Anna sent me to help you get ready for dinner."

Ida tried to protest but the maid just waved her arguments aside.

"I'm Alice, by the way." Alice walked over to the dresses lying across the bed and studied them thoughtfully.

Finally she looked up at Ida, "M'lady, would you be so kind as to go behind the dressing screen." Nervously Ida ambled behind the dressing screen.

Alice then slipped her the dress that she had picked her.

Ida fingered the smooth side of the overlay of her dress as

Alice did her hair in perfect curls. The longer she sat there, Ida became more and more nervous every second that passed by.

Finally, Alice murmured, "There, you look perfect." Ida stood up slowly and anxiously walked to a mirror.

She gawked at her appearance, "Oh Alice, how could I ever thank you enough."

The maid suddenly gasped as if she had just realized something for the first time, "The prince will soon be here to escort you to the parlor and then dinner." A quick knock sounded on the door and Alice's eyes widened along with Ida's. Peter was escorting her to dinner. Why had no one bothered to tell her before now!

Ida, sick to her stomach, walked over to the door. She looked back at Alice who motioned for her to go on.

Ida took a deep breath, put her hand on the doorknob, and then slowly twisted it. She pulled the door open to find Peter looking like a prince and not the pirate she had known him as. She sat terrified, as the impertinent man stared at her face.

Finally, he seemed to realize what he had been doing and cleared his throat after blushing almost as crimson as her dress. "Lady Id-Diana I am here to escort you to the parlor, and then dinner."

6 ERIKA

During dinner, Erika sat next to the Princess Annarealia while Ida was placed next to Peter.

"Tell me girls, how exactly did you happen upon the chance of meeting our dear Peter?"

Momentarily stunned, Erika sat silently as she twisted the fabric of her skirt in her hands. She couldn't answer the question; she didn't know how to respond.

Luckily, for the first time, Ida spoke before Erika had the chance to make a fool of herself, "My sister and I were on our way to stay with our mother's sister who resides in London. We were going to stay with her until the ball." Ida paused for a moment, "As we approached London, we heard gunshots outside the carriage. It was highwaymen m'lady. If it were not for your son, we would surely be dead. He then offered to help us explain the situation to you and now we're here."

The queen looked horrified. As she was about to say something, the servants began to enter the room with the dinner's first course. A mouthwatering aroma enveloped the grand chamber as bowls of soup were set before the small group.

"Let us eat." The king announced.

Erika noticed that while they were eating, Peter would secretly glance at Ida whenever he believed no one was looking. Then when she believed no one would notice, Ida would glare at the crown prince even though it was a terrible thing to do with him being the crown prince and all. Erika ate in silent amusement all throughout the next four courses of the meal.

That night Erika lay comfortably in bed for the first time in days. The next day she awoke to find the maid, Lydia, putting a tray of food on a small table next to the wardrobe.

"Good morning m'lady. Princess Anna has requested your presence after dinner. She would like you to attend to the royal seamstress with her to be measured for your ball gown."

Erika smiled at the thought of a ball gown in her near future, and then frowned when she realized why she needed the dress in the first place. She wouldn't be in this position if the Captain hadn't captured Ida and herself. She was only following his orders so she would see her family again, and in this life, not the next.

She sat up and her hand shot to the gold locket around her neck instinctively. She glanced at the tray her borrowed ladies maid had brought her, suddenly sick at the sight of the food.

Her thoughts turned to her birthday. It had been only a week ago, but felt as if it had been years since she had seen her family. She would see them again, she knew it. That day they had no way of knowing what was to come.

Her sweet twin brothers had been so excited to celebrate the occasion. Her frail grandmother had given her most prized possession to her. She missed every one of them. Most of all, she missed her parents.

Erika lost her train of thought as Lydia dropped a clay water pitcher onto the floor with a loud crash. She ran to help the maid while muttering, "It's fine. All's well."

After the pieces of the broken pitcher had been cleaned up Lydia excused herself to go take care of the clay shards. Erika sluggishly walked to the wardrobe. She gazed at all the dresses borrowed from the Duchess of Cornwall's daughter, the lady Lucille Lockhart. Who was also staying until the ball.

Instantaneously a sky blue dress caught her eye. When Erika had put the dress on Lydia appeared again and began to tame Erika's monstrous hair. Lydia tried all sorts of hairstyles but only one actually looked presentable. So, Erika found herself walking beside Princess Anna with her hair in an orderly chignon.

They walked through the corridors of the palace until they came to a wooden door near the servant's quarters.

Anna knocked lightly on the door then waited for a musical voice to call, "Come in." They walked into a bright spacious room. Inside was a girl about fifteen years of age putting colorful fabrics on a shelf across the room. "Princess Annarealia, it is so good to see you."

The girl shoved the rest of the fabrics she had in her arms onto the already full shelf, then ran and gave the Princess a small curtsy.

Anna nodded back at the girl then looked towards Erika, "Lady Eleanor this is London's best seamstress, Marianne Alpine. Marianne this is Lady Eleanor."

Marianne smiled sweetly at Erika, "It is very nice to meet you."

Erika smiled, "And it's very nice to meet you."

The seamstress turned to Anna, "What can I do for you?"

Anna glanced at Erika, "We need you to create two beautiful ball gowns before the ball. One for Lady Eleanor, and the other for her sister Lady Diana. Do you think you are up for the challenge?"

Marianne thought for a second before responding, "I can most definitely try to make two ball gowns in such little time."

Erika and Anna beamed, "Oh thank you Marianne, I hope we don't take too much of your time, but I was hoping you could measure Eleanor today and Diana tomorrow." Anna said nervously.

Marianne giggled, "Of course I can fit them into my schedule." Erika and Anna both sighed in relief. Marianne walked down a hallway and motioned for the two girls to follow her. The pair followed the hallway to a cozy room with pastel blue and yellow walls.

Marianne was in the corner mumbling to herself and going through drawers within a cupboard. She turned and said, "Eleanor will you please stand still with your arms horizontally out?" Erika as she was told while Marianne measured her. Finally the seamstress stepped away and said, "There, I have all that I need. Now we need to discuss the color of the dress. I was thinking a deep purple or a lighter shade of blue."

Anna looked at Erika, "I believe I like the idea of a light blue gown."

"Excellent choice." Said Marianne, "What do you think Eleanor?"

"Yes, I believe I would like the gown to be blue." Said Erika.

After discussing all of the details involving the dress, Anna and Erika left Marianne to her work. Out in the corridor Anna lead Erika towards a door with painted gold flowers on it.

Anna stopped, "This is called the flos hortus room, or flower garden in Latin." She pushed the door open, "We call it this because it is an indoor greenhouse."

Erika gawked at all the flowers. She walked around and found her favorite flowers. She leaned down and pushed her nose into a pastel yellow rose and breathed in the extraordinarily sweet fragrance. Erika stood up and saw Anna smelling some dusty pink tulips a few steps away.

Anna saw the awed look on Erika's face and said, "I know, it's breathtaking. My father built this place for my mother when she became sick of winter. It was supposed to be a place of everlasting summer." Erika looked around again and sighed happily. Anna's face suddenly brightened, "We should pick bouquets of flowers to put around the castle!"

So the two girls spent the rest of the day picking flowers and inserting them all over the castle. This day was one of the first days since she had been kidnapped that Erika actually felt a little joy.

7 IDA

Ida spent the day in the library reading and deciding if their foolish plan would truly work or not. After dinner she secretly met Erika and Peter in the flos hortus room to discuss ways to complete the plan. They had managed to get inside the castle but had no idea of how to get away with stealing the crown.

Ida thought about how much she wanted to see her family. She hoped they could think of how to steal the crown soon or she would never see them again. Only then would Erika be her only family left. She glanced at Erika and Peter who seemed just as discouraged as she felt.

"What if we steal the crown before the ball?" Said Ida. Erika and Peter pondered the idea.

Peter leaned forward, "Wouldn't that be too risky? The queen would be in her chambers preparing for the ball hours before it begins." Peter was right. They couldn't do it before the ball.

"Well." Said Ida, "Maybe we should continue this conversation in the morning." They agreed then all went their separate ways.

That night the trio went to sleep restlessly and still without a plan. The next day after breakfast Anna took Ida to Marianne's quarters to take her measurements and decide on the dress details.

Ida stood with her arms out thinking about how serious Peter was all the time.

"Lady Diana, Lady Diana." Ida realized Marianne was speaking to her.

"Sorry I was woolgathering."

"Lady Diana we were wondering if you like the color red for your dress?"

Ida thought for a minute, "Red will be perfect." After the girls had decided on a dress color and style it was almost time for dinner.

Ida hurried to her chamber to change and have Alice fix her hair. She whisked her wardrobe doors open. She quickly chose a dark blue evening gown to wear then went to change behind a screen while Alice went to get water to wash Ida's face. Ida came out from behind the screen to see Alice picking a piece of paper off the floor. She gave the paper to Ida.

Ida saw the note was addressed to her. She had no time to stop and read the note so she set it on her make-up table. Ida washed her face in the water Alice had brought. Alice then hurriedly did her hair in curled tendrils then Ida rushed out the door and down the hallway.

She was walking so quickly when she was near the stairs she bumped into a figure. Momentarily stunned she stumbled sideways until her foot no longer touched the floor. She screamed then a hand grabbed her hand before she could fall down the stairs. Her vision cleared and she saw the person that had saved her from falling down the grand staircase. Peter stared at her smirking in an irritating way.

Ida frowned then said, "Are you going to just sit there staring, or are you going to help me up?" Peter pulled her onto solid ground then began to laugh. Ida silently slipped away down the hallway towards the dining room embarrassed.

During dinner every time Ida looked at Peter the memory of her almost falling consumed her; so when everyone had finished eating she excused herself and hurried to her room.

She got to her quarters and promptly collapsed against the door. Her face reddened as she thought of the incident before dinner. Then she sat at her make-up table and started to brush her hair. When she finished brushing her hair she finally saw the note she had placed on her table.

Her hand instinctively opened the note and it read. Dear lady Diana, meet me in the flos hortus room at exactly midnight tonight. The note had no signature on it. Ida wondered who could have sent the mysterious letter.

Without warning the door opened and she quickly hid the letter in the pocket of her dress. Alice meandered into the room carrying something with a large cloth covering it. Ida gazed at it curiously wondering what it could be.

Alice laid the bundle onto the bed then gently pulled the cloth off of it. Ida gasped in surprise; she had never seen a more beautiful gown. She walked towards the gown as if in a dream, then fingered the smooth silk fabric. It really was the most breathtaking dress she had ever seen.

As a Baron's daughter she had grown up wearing extravagant dresses but none of her finest gowns could compare to the creation on the bed. How Marianne had created the dress in so little time was a mystery, she had clearly put a lot of time into it.

Alice carefully put the dress in the wardrobe. She then asked if she could help Ida any further.

Ida dismissed the maid after assuring her there was nothing more for her to do that Ida could not do for herself.

Ida then glanced out the window at the London tower to see what time it was. The colossal clock read five minutes to twelve. She hurried and put on a white borrowed shawl, grabbed a lit candle, then quietly whisked out of the room. She glided through the halls like a ghost until she came to the door of the flos hortus room. She took a deep breath then slowly opened the door.

Inside the chamber was the same lady the group had encountered in Aldeburgh. The same lady the Captain had been afraid of.

Ida glanced at the door ready to run at any moment. She put the candle down on the floor beside her.

The lady smiled sadly as she strolled towards Ida, "Ida my dear, I am so sorry for your loss."

Confused Ida asked, "Who are you, and what loss are you talking about?"

The lady's smile faltered, "My dear I am Victoria, your aunt."

Ida reeled back at the sudden information. Then, she asked again, "What loss?"

"Well of course William didn't tell you or your sister." Victoria muttered then almost tearfully replied in a choked voice,

"When William, or the Captain as you would call him, captured you and your sister, he didn't just leave the rest of your family alone. Instead, he killed them one by one. My sister was the first to face his wrath."

Shocked, Ida fell to her knees in despair. She sobbed freely as Victoria stroked her hair. She then came to the conclusion that the Captain had been a worse person than she had realized. She had had no reason to follow the Captain's orders, he had blackmailed her saying he would kill her family if she did not do what he told her. But, her family had already been dead; she had protected no one by following orders.

Ida looked up at Victoria who did not seem like the killer that Ida had expected. The Captain had been scared of her after all. But why was the question? She stood up with Victoria's help then they both sat on a bench carved out of marble.

Her aunt gave her a hug then said, "I'm sorry everything wasn't what you thought it was. But I also need to tell you that the reason the Captain wants the three magical items is because he wants to become king of the nation of Avaria, not because of whatever lies he has told you."

Ida tried to process all of the new information, "How should we go about stealing the tiara, and what do I do about Peter, he doesn't know about you right?"

Victoria grinned, "Don't worry about him, he's my spy. His mission is to protect you girls from William. Him getting to go with you and Erika to retrieve the tiara is a bonus and will help our side in this war of survival. Peter and my associate that you will meet at the ball tomorrow will know what to do."

"How will I know who your associate is?" Asked Ida.

Victoria reached into the pocket of her dress and pulled out a silver metal bracelet with a lily carved into it. "My associate will be wearing this. Now I must leave you but I shall see you and your sister very soon. I promise."

Victoria then walked to the large window, waved goodbye to Ida, and then promptly slid out into the streets. Ida stared out into the night as the cool wind enveloped the room causing her candle to flicker out leaving her in darkness.

8 ERIKA

Erika woke up after a night full of endless nightmares. However, the morning light calmed her.

Sylvia came into the room with a tray heaping with food.

"Good morning m'lady. I am to tell you the ball will begin promptly at six o'clock tonight."

"Thank you Lydia. You may take your leave." Said Erika. Lydia set the tray on the small table in the room, curtsied, and then left without another word.

Erika slowly got out of bed and made her way over to the window. She watched the dark gray clouds on the horizon travel slowly towards the city. The developing storm appeared to be heralding an irrevocably dark future. She knew her life was about to change more than it already had. She just didn't know if she was ready for it.

Erika forced herself to turn back towards her breakfast even though the aroma of it had begun to make her nauseous. She sat in the chair by the small table and compelled herself to eat so Lydia would not become suspicious of her loss of appetite.

After eating half of her food Erika rang for Lydia then proceeded to get dressed. Lydia came and went as she took the tray back to the kitchens. She then appeared again to help Erika with her hair. As the maid brushed her flaming locks Erika thought about how weird it was to get ready for the day, but only a few hours after to completely change appearances for the ball. Lydia finished and Erika was off to the library to find any books on

William Hilyard.

    When she got to the library she found Ida, who was reading a gothic novel and enjoying her last few moments of peace before their journey began. Erika tapped on her sister's shoulder. Ida jumped with alarm then sighed in relief.

    "Erika, I need to tell you about something that happened last night." Her voice grew quiet and shaky as she told Erika everything that had happened while everyone had been asleep. Ida's voice cracked as she told Erika that all of their family was dead except for their mysterious aunt Victoria. When Ida finished talking her sister's face was pale white.

    Erika took a deep breath as she held back tears, "So, we bring the tiara to Victoria. Then what? We have no other family; we'll be dragged into a war that doesn't concern us. We'll have to side and fight with Victoria."

    Ida nodded gravely, "You're right. There is nothing else we can do, so we must fight whether we want to or not." All of a sudden the library doors burst open revealing Anna.

    "There you girls are. I came to tell you that lunch is ready and after we eat we shall pick flowers from the flos hortus room to weave in our hair for the ball!"

    Erika and Ida tried their hardest to fake vivacity at the idea as they followed Anna to the dining room, but the girls couldn't hide all of their heartache behind counterfeit smiles. They quickly ate a small lunch then hurried to the flos hortus room.

    Erika walked slowly through the rows of vibrant flowers that didn't seem as colorful anymore. She glanced at Anna's basket full of pink carnations, and Ida's bursting with unique scarlet peonies. They had been looking at flowers for nearly two hours and Erika had yet to find some that matched her dress.

    A flash of white caught her eye across the room and she turned to find the perfect flower, white roses. She carefully picked the flowers then the three girls parted ways to prepare for the ball.

    When she got to her room Sylvia had laid her dress out but was nowhere to be seen. She walked to her makeup table to take the pins out of her hair. As she laid one on the table she took notice of a small piece of paper for the first time. As it was addressed to her she read it.

    The note gave her the information that Victoria's associate

had made contact with Peter and had told him how they were to steal the tiara. She stared at the words hopeful.

All of the sudden Sylvia came into the room out of breath, "I'm so sorry I'm late my lady." Erika hurriedly hid the note in the folds of her skirt and then when Sylvia turned away from her, in the drawer of the dressing table.

"It's all right we still have plenty of time to prepare for the ball," Erika stood up and walked towards the changing screen, "shall we begin?"

Sylvia nodded and gave a little smile, she then handed Erika her ball gown. As she was changing Erika examined and grew fond of her new beautiful dress. She slipped it over her head and watched as the silky skirt fell to the ground. The skirt of the dress faded from white to azure blue reminding her of a wave on the sea.

She hesitantly came out from behind the screen, afraid of what she might look like in the dress. She felt as if she wasn't worthy to wear it after all of the horrible things the Captain had made her do.

When Sylvia first saw Erika her mouth went into an O shape.

"What? Does it look bad?" Erika shifted her weight from side to side as she waited for an answer.

"No m'lady, on the contrary. It looks beautiful on you."

Erika sighed in relief as she turned to sit at her make-up table. Sylvia began to brush her hair. They talked little as Sylvia pulled half of Erika's hair into a bun towards the back of her head then curled the rest in tight ringlets.

As Sylvia finished her hair Erika grew more nervous every second. This would be her first ball and she was only going so she could help steal the Queen of England's tiara.

"There... I'm all finished." Said Sylvia proudly.

Erika stared at herself in the mirror. Tonight her hair looked darker and less orange. It seemed to be an alluring color of copper. Her hair genuinely looked pretty with the porcelain roses she had picked woven into the bun in her hair.

She took a shaky breath then walked to the door; she heard the music in the ballroom begin revealing the start of the ball. She looked back at Sylvia who gave her a small encouraging smile, then slowly opened the door.

She exited her room then strolled through the large hallways until she came to the grand staircase that led to the large ballroom. She cautiously stepped down the stairs, concentrating on not stepping and tripping on her long skirts.

Once in the crush of people she set out to find someone she knew. She wandered around until she found Anna and Peter talking to each other on the outskirts of the room. She looked around to see if Ida was with or around them but could not find her sister. She went to stand by the Prince and Princess.

"Have you seen my sister?"

Anna and Peter shook their heads as the room suddenly went quiet. Everyone's heads turned towards the staircase. The crowd then began to whisper to each other.

Erika turned to see what had caused all of the commotion and gasped in surprise. Ida glided down the stairs in her breathtaking scarlet gown a scandalous color in a sea of dull colored gowns. The peonies expertly woven in the half of her hair in a bun made it look even thicker and shinier than ever. Young men flocked around Ida hoping to be lucky enough to be rewarded with a dance. Peter made his excuses then went to join the hopeful with a fixed look on his face.

Poor Ida was shy and hated the attention she had put upon herself, Erika could just see the way her sister twirled the front piece of her hair in anxiety which the men mistook as flirting.

"The poor girl looks as if she might faint."

Erika turned to agree with Anna.

They were then approached by a woman.

"Oh... Lady Eleanor, let me introduce Lady Emilia Gordon, the Countess of Dorset."

Erika curtsied and exchanged the usual pleasantries before excusing herself from the conversation. She then went to look for Victoria's associate.

As she walked a pretty blonde girl around her age fell into step beside her.

"Are you Erika Fillmore?" She asked.

"Yes." Said Erika as she noticed the bracelet on the girl's arm. It was silver with a lily carved into it. It was a perfect match to the bracelet Ida had described Victoria's associate would wear.

"Would you fancy a little fresh air?" Asked the girl.

"Fresh air would be lovely." Replied Erika.

They made their way outside and started around the gardens. The girl stopped walking as soon as they were out of sight from the rest of the partygoers. She slipped her hand into the pocket of her dress and pulled out what was inside.

In her hand was a silver tiara with a beautiful carved feather in the center surrounded by rubies. Erika's eyes widened at the sight of it.

"Who are you and however did you manage to get this?"

The girl frowned, "My name is Taria, I work as a spy for Victoria. We don't have the time for me to explain what I did to get this. The Captain knows you have betrayed him and is coming for the feather. We need to find Peter and Ida and leave before it is too late."

Taria grabbed Erika's hand and half dragged her back to the ballroom before Erika could register the new information. As they reached the entrance to the ballroom Taria said, "You find Ida and I'll find Peter."

They then parted ways and Erika frantically began to search for her Ida. She found her sister by Anna talking to Lady Emilia Gordon. Lady Emilia was telling Anna and Ida about how she had sprained her ankle last spring when Erika interrupted her.

"Princess Annarealia, Lady Emilia, I am sorry to barge into your conversation but I need to speak to my sister.

Both the Princess and the Lady Emilia said they understood, so Erika and Ida wandered away from the two ladies. Erika leaned closer to Ida to keep the surrounding people from hearing their conversation.

"Ida we must leave, Victoria's associate has hold of the tiara. But the Captain knows we have betrayed him and is coming for us. The associate has gone to find Peter. We must find them then leave."

Ida's expression which had been joyful a moment ago was now downtrodden and fearful. She nodded and the two girls went in search of their companions.

They found Peter and Taria in a corner of the room in the middle of a heated whispered argument. Before they saw the sisters Erika heard Peter whisper, "That doesn't explain why you are here" before he quit talking and acknowledged the two girls.

"Are we interrupting anything?"

"No, you didn't interrupt us we were just making a plan."

Erika knew this wasn't true but stayed silent anyways.

Peter went on, "We must leave quickly and be careful that no one sees us go." He looked around to make sure no one was paying attention to them, "Follow me."

Nervously Erika followed Peter and Taria with Ida right behind her. Peter led them through the ballroom and out into the hallway. Peter pulled one of the tapestries off the wall to reveal a door that they then went through.

Peter turned around to speak to them, "This passage leads to the stable where we can get horses for the journey ahead of us."

Erika tried to look around the passage but the only light was from candles spaced apart from one another along the walls. Her ball gown brushed against both sides of the narrow tunnel and made her all the more conscious of the smell of wet soil and mold seeping out of the dirt walls. The party continued on for a short while. Before coming to a ladder leading up to a trapdoor.

Peter climbed the ladder then tried to quietly open the trapdoor but it let out a high pitched whistle as it swung open.

"Someone would have heard that." Muttered Peter and the others began to panic a little. They all climbed the ladder and out the trapdoor as fast as possible. Taria stood watch while Peter, Erika, and Ida began to saddle four horses. They were finishing as Taria ran towards them, "Somebody is coming."

Erika tried to remember if she had saddled Ida's horse correctly as they mounted the horses but lost her train of thought as the stable doors burst open. The four companions raced their horses through the doors without looking to see who was after them. Erika heard horses behind them and urged her horse to run faster.

They dashed through the open palace gates and into the streets of London. The loud cobblestone streets made it impossible for them to lose the people behind them. Heavy rain started to pour down on them and thunder rumbled as lightning lit the sky.

The city of London finally came to an end revealing a large forest which they galloped into. Erika looked back in time to see the horses of whoever had been chasing them rear and refuse to cross into the wilderness.

    The four companions wouldn't stop; their horses ran madly through the forest. As they slowed to a canter all of a sudden a deafening crack of thunder sounded. Ida's horse reared and her saddle broke. She went tumbling through the air into a tree with a resounding thud. Erika quickly jumped off her horse and ran to Ida who lay unconscious on the ground.

9 IDA

Ida woke up to a large portion of her right arm bandaged in white cloth from her elbow to her shoulder. Erika sat next to her and Peter and Taria sat across from her around a fire. In the dim firelight she sat up and saw her left leg also bandaged through a slit in her dress and stockings. She looked up at the stars shimmering across the night sky wondering how long she had been unconscious. Erika was the first person to notice she was awake.

"Ida, you're awake." Peter and Taria looked to her as they also noticed she had awoken.

"Ah, Ida, I was just going to tell Erika the history between the Captain and Victoria." Said Peter.

Ida nodded for him to go on so he began, "Victoria was once a Princess of Avaria, an island off the coast of France. And the Captain was a general in the nation's army. The two fell in love against the King and Queen's wishes. They planned to elope but in a sudden turn of events the Captain became power hungry. Everyone believes it is because Victoria wasn't next in line for the crown. Instead the role of Queen passed to her sister Elaine Price, your mother. The Captain was furious when he found out who was next in line for the crown. Avaria is famous for its mass of pirates that roam the cities and take refuge there. And that is what the Captain became, a pirate. He now has plans of taking the island by force and becoming King. There are only two people in his way." He paused for a minute, "Those two people are you girls. Victoria has renounced the throne and only reins while Ida is not on the island, if Ida fails to rule Erika is next in line. This is the reason your parents never told you about your mother's heritage. They didn't want you to know what may happen to you and decided to give you a childhood in which would make up for the hardships the future would bring you."

Ida began to feel ill. She grabbed Erika's arm to steady herself even though she was sitting down. She was to be Queen of an island she had never heard of.

"If I am to be Queen why did the Captain murder the rest of our family, or us for that matter of fact?"

Peter sighed in remorse, "Your father could never have been King due to not being of royal blood and your mother had already renounced the throne. The crown only passes through the female bloodline so your brothers would have never qualified for the crown. And your grandmother had witnessed the Captain capturing you and was sentenced to death for that reason. And I do not know why the Captain has kept you alive."

Ida lay back down and closed her eyes. She couldn't cry over her family anymore, now instead of being sad she felt only emptiness. They died because of me she thought over and over again. She heard the others prepare for bed as she began to think of her future. Would the Captain try to kill her and Erika next? Would he succeed? These thoughts ran through her head until she finally drifted to sleep.

The next morning Ida awoke to hear birds chirping and see the sunrise bask everything in a warm orange glow. She stood slowly, careful not to put any weight on her injured leg or arm. Her companions were all asleep so she decided to explore the forest around her. She walked around the trees and through bushes wincing every time her left foot made contact with the ground.

Her once beautiful ball gown was now ragged and torn causing it to snag on everything. After meandering through the thick growth she finally heard the faint noise of a stream. She ran towards the sound hoping she was going the right way.

As she went through the night before she struggled to keep her tears in check. As she reached the bank of a steam she let go of her emotions. She fell to the ground and sobbed as she thought of her family and how the Captain had killed them. She cried and cried until she had no more tears to cry.

When she finally calmed down she unwrapped the bandages on her leg and arm painstakingly slow. She winced as dried blood stuck to the cloth pulled on the wounds and made them bleed once more. White pus seeped out of the cut on her leg. She averted her gaze the best she could as she lowered her leg into the stream. She bit her lip in an attempt to quiet her scream of pain as the water cleaned the wound the best it could. She finished then repeated the process with her arm. After cleaning the wounds she ripped cloth off of the underdress she wore and rebandaged her arm and leg.

She stood slowly then began to limp back the way she had come. Ida limped about fifteen feet before she began to feel faint. The ground seemed to sway and she bumped into a tree. Something began to drip down her leg. She looked down to see the bandage soaked through and blood slowly making its way down to her ankle.

She kept limping forward as she heard a noise in the distance that was becoming louder with each second. Her foot hit a tree root and her leg erupted into blazing pain. She fell face first onto the ground then turned onto her back. The world began to fade in and out. A person appeared above her, she thought it was Peter but wasn't sure until her vision cleared a little. The person picked her up then all went black.

Once again Ida woke to find Erika beside her. Her sister looked terrible with red tearstained eyes.

"What has happened?" Ida asked feverishly.

Erika quickly turned to look at Ida then began to cry.

"The wounds on your arm and leg have... have infection in them. You've had a high fever all day and Peter says you'll only live a few hours depending on how fast the infection spreads into your blood."

Peter and Taria noticed Ida was awake and came over by the girls.

"I think we might have a way to ensure Ida doesn't die." Said Peter as he took the tiara out of the hole in the ground they had put it in to hide it. "The Captain said that the phoenix feather is supposed to heal people."

"Yes," Said Erika, "but how can we trust the Captain or anything he has said? For all we know the feather could kill Ida!"

Taria joined in, "Perhaps we should let Ida decide? It's her life after all."

Everyone's attention turned to Ida. She thought a moment before saying weakly, "I'll do it."

Peter nodded then handed the tiara to her. They all waited not knowing how it worked. Suddenly it erupted in a white blazing fire that began to surround Ida. Everyone jumped back and Ida screamed hoarsely and tried to throw the tiara but was too weak. It seemed to be sucking what was left of her life out of her. Then, the feather and tiara separated and the part that was the tiara disappeared. The fire continued to spread over Ida until the flames covered her completely. Her companions watched in horror as the flames died out leaving Ida looking dazed.

Erika ran to her sister to make sure she was alright. Ida unraveled her bandages to reveal that her wounds had been completely healed and had not even left scars.

The feather, she noticed, instead of silver was now a shiny bronze. Ida picked it up; it felt as cool as metal but soft like a real feather. Erika watched her nervously as she stood carefully. She was amazed as she felt no pain. Now able to comprehend stuff clearly Ida looked around the camp.

"Where did the horses go?" She asked confused.

"When we went to help you after you had been thrown from your horse they were scared away by the thunder. We had just enough time to grab the tiara before they ran."

After this experience, the party began to plan where they would go now.

Later that day the sun began to set enveloping the trees in pink and orange hues. Ida wandered a little ways away and sat on a decomposing log half hidden by a tree. She reflected on all that had happened. She thought about her family and the servants and guards that had died trying to save them. Her hand went to her pocket as she thought about the feather and how it had saved her life. Her mind then went to her companions.

Erika could make the worst of situations seem easy to endure, Peter could charm his way out of anything, and Taria's quick wit could win any battle. What had she to offer to their group? So far she had only managed to get injured and panic in most circumstances.

Ida was lost in thought when Erika came and sat next to her.

"Ida..."

"Yes?"

"Do you ever question who to trust? I mean... do you truly believe Victoria is our aunt?"

Ida turned to face her sister, "You have not seen Victoria but the resemblance between her and mother is uncanny. Their noses and mouths are shaped the same and they both have eyes the color of sapphires. How could she not be our aunt?"

Ida stood and walked back towards camp confused that Erika could be so naive to think that Victoria wasn't their aunt. She walked over to Peter and Taria who was going over the fastest route to Avaria.

"How are we going to get to Avaria?" Asked Ida. Peter traced his finger along a makeshift map drawn in the dirt.

"We'll travel south to Brighton where Victoria will be waiting for us."

Glad to have a plan Ida spent the rest of the day preparing to travel to Brighton. That night the sound of wolves howling echoed throughout the forest as Ida looked up at the shimmering stars. She wondered if her family was watching over her as her guardian angels. She hoped they were proud of her.

Her thoughts then rather strangely turned to Peter. She had been mortified when she had first awoken from being thrown from the horse and able to remember most of what had happened. Her stockings had been ripped open in order for her companions to bandage her wound and it was not a question of who had done it. She also knew Peter had been the one to carry her back to their camp after she had fainted from sickness. And she hated it; she hated thinking about him when there were things more dire to prevail upon.

Around her the cricket's sang their lullaby and Ida's eyelids began to hang heavy. She took one last look at the dying remains of the fire in the darkness, willed her thoughts to be silent, then slowly drifted to sleep.

10 ERIKA

Erika glanced back through the dense forest as she ran. The Captain raced after her yelling death threats. One by one Ida, Peter, and Taria joined the Captain. Her foot suddenly struck a tree root and sent her tumbling to the ground. The Captain and her companions surrounded her and she scrambled to her feet. The ground beneath her then crumbled leaving her to fall into a dark abyss.

She awoke to Ida shaking her lightly, her brow damp with a cold sweat.

"Are you alright?" Her sister asked concerned, "You were calling out in your sleep."

"I'm fine."

Ida gave her a small smile then returned to where she had been before by Peter and Taria. To reassure herself that the ground wouldn't crumble beneath her Erika stood slowly. She rubbed the sleep out of her eyes, grabbed the saddle blanket she had slept on, and then joined her companions who were waiting for her so they could leave.

She glanced back at the ground she had slept on before turning and starting the long journey ahead of her.

Erika and her companions walked for what felt like an eternity. As they had begun Erika's footsteps had been full of energy, almost like she had been dancing through the forest. But now her feet dragged on the ground in her broken shoes that were starting to give her blisters.

Peter had assured them that they could possibly walk to Brighton in about a day and a half but her feet hurt so much that she didn't know how much farther she could go.

She looked down at her tattered dress and wondered if they were near any villages at all. When she looked up the trees in front of her suddenly came to an end revealing a small town.

They watched as wagons and carriages drifted in and out of the town. Erika had an idea and began to smile a little mischievously, "I think that two of us should go into town and the other two of us stay here. How about Taria and I go and get supplies while Ida and Peter stay?"

Everyone nodded in approval of her plan except Ida who clearly didn't want to stay with Peter. Ida smiled sweetly.

"Erika may I talk to you in private." She said more as a command than a question.

Erika's confidence in her plan faltered a bit, "Of course." Ida took Erika by the arm and dragged her a little ways away from Peter and Taria.

"Why must you leave me with Peter when you know I wish for good conversation?"

"Please just stay with him. We wouldn't be gone long and I don't want you to be placed in unsafe circumstances."

Ida folded her arms then sighed, "Alright... I'll stay. But you better be back soon."

Erika smiled in relief as they rejoined Peter and Taria who were arguing once again but stopped once they saw the sisters coming near them.

Erika looked to Taria, "We should go." Taria nodded in a reply. Peter handed them some coins he had stolen from the palace then they left. As they left the safety of the forest, Erika turned back to see Ida glaring at her as Peter attempted to begin a conversation. She turned away laughing at the scene her sister portrayed.

As they entered the town Erika looked down at her dress feeling completely out of place. All the townspeople dressed in simple clothes dyed different shades of browns and grays which blended in perfectly with the houses and shops lining the street. She and Taria were dressed as ragged peacocks in comparison.

The smell of food drifting in the air made Erika's stomach

growl. The girls roamed through the few streets of the town trying to find shops that sold what they needed.

"Taria... why are you and Peter always arguing?"

Taria glared at her, "That is none of your business." She whispered fiercely.

"Well I thought that if we are to be allies we might as well get to know one another since you might one day save my life."

Taria grunted then turned to face her, "If you must know, about a year ago, Peter and I were betrothed to one another. But that was when I still thought of myself as the lady Tariana Aniston the daughter of the Duke and Duchess of Knightley. On the wedding day it suddenly struck me that I didn't want to be stuck in a loveless marriage; and I certainly didn't love Peter. So I ran away and shortened my name to Taria. A month later Victoria found me starving and near death with illness. She nursed me back to health then when I was strong enough she taught me how to fight and I became her thief in a way. I stole meaningless objects for her. I didn't even know that Peter was Victoria's spy until he was assigned to spy on the Captain six months ago." Taria stopped to wipe away a few stray tears, "Now my past has come back to haunt me."

Erika watched as one of the most resilient people she had ever known showed vulnerability. She didn't mind, everyone cried a little every now and then. She smiled kindly.

"I don't think Peter blames you for not wanting to marry him. He probably didn't want to live unhappily for the rest of his life just as much as you didn't. Now, I think he fancies Ida more than anything. It's only a matter of time before my clueless sister figures it out. She's dead set on believing he is a complete bore."

The two laughed together.

"Come we must find what supplies we can before Ida decides to come and yell at us for taking so long."

They then continued to roam through the town buying what supplies they could find. When they found most everything they needed they exited the town.

They found Peter and Ida both laughing uncontrollably.

"I see you two warmed up to each other." Erika said while smiling. "Here put these on." She gave them the clothes and shoes she and Taria had purchased. All four of them went different ways into the forest to change.

When they got back they ate some of the food they had bought. After half an hour they then started to walk once more. They walked until the sun began to set low in the sky then decided to stop for the night.

As Erika and Ida gathered firewood Erika said, "Have you had a change of heart towards Peter?"

Ida smiled shyly, "I think so. I don't find him as bad as I once did." Erika grinned glad her sister's cold heart had begun to thaw.

"What were the two of you laughing about when Taria and I came back from buying supplies?"

"Peter was telling me stories of him growing up in the palace and of working as Victoria's spy." Ida blushed and played with her hair. Erika knew her matchmaking was working.

"We better hurry, the sooner we collect all the wood, the sooner you can get back to your beloved." Said Erika jokingly.

"He is not my beloved... we are barely friends and nothing more, and that is how it will always be." Ida said the last part sadly.

Erika knew her sister meant that Peter would never come to love her, which was simply not true, "Fine... but we really should hurry I'm starving after all that walking." The girls finished collecting the wood and went back to camp to start a fire.

They got back to find Peter and Taria not arguing which was unusual and a nice change to how things were most of the time. After they started a small fire they each ate their small portion of dinner. That night the group told stories and joked around with one another which was an alteration to the tension that was usually so thick you could cut it with a knife.

As the fire grew dim Peter cleared his throat, "We should be to Brighton sometime tomorrow. But we'll have to cross a river to get there so everyone get some rest for the journey ahead."

They then went to find someplace on the ground comfortable enough to sleep on.

Erika sat on the ground beneath a tree. She took off her shoes to relieve some of the pain in her feet. Crickets chirped wildly. As she lay down she saw a glimpse of the stars through the thick canopy of leaves and tree branches. The last thing she heard before drifting asleep was the wind howling softly through the forest.

The start of the next day was similar to the one before. They ate breakfast then began to walk again. They soon arrived at the river Peter had warned them about the night before. The water was ice cold to the touch and flowed deeper into the forest out of view.

They decided that to be safe, Peter would carry each of the girls to the other side of the river. Erika went first. She lifted her skirts to not get them wet as Peter picked her up as if she was as light as a feather then set out across the river. After a minute they arrived at the bank of the far side of the river.

Peter set her down then she watched as he crossed back to the other side and carried Taria across then went back for Ida. Erika watched as Peter said something to Ida that made her turn away to hide her red face and begin to toy with her hair nervously. Erika recognized a spark between them; she only hoped they acknowledged it before it was too late.

When Peter and Ida finally reached the other side Ida quickly walked away from him.

"We're almost to Brighton there's only maybe five more miles to go." Said Peter as he shivered slightly.

So, they continued on. Finally they reached the town. Erika was relieved; soon she would have a home and family again. All she had to do was find Victoria's ship.

"Peter, Taria, what is Victoria's ship named?"

"It's called Greed's Venture. We'll have to split up, there are three different piers and it could be docked at any of them." Said Peter.

Erika was given the feather for safe keeping and then they split up. Erika and Taria were on their own while Peter and Ida went together, for the safety of the future Queen of course.

On her way to her assigned pier, Erika marveled at the town's beauty. All of the architecture was enchanting and the citizen's gardens were just as breathtaking.

At last she arrived at the eastern pier. The smell of the ocean was overwhelming as she scanned through the few ships scattered in the water. Her breath caught in her throat as she took notice of one ship in particular. Along the pier lay the Siren's

Chanty.

    She had to tell the others! The Captain was here in Brighton. She turned to go find her companions but found her path blocked by Rotten John, the Captain's vile henchman. The Captain appeared from behind Rotten John, his cutlass in his hand.

    "Well, well, well, if it isn't the little traitor. Where's your friends now little Princess?"

    Erika's knees went weak and began to shake, "You'll... you'll never find them!" The Captain laughed his signature grating laugh.

    "What are you going to do to stop me? Fight me?" He laughed again.

    Erika admitted to herself that she could never beat him; she was almost a full foot shorter than his six feet. The Captain gave a hand signal to Rotten John. The henchman searched her and found the feather in the pocket of her dress. He then tied her hands behind her back and gagged her.

    Tears began to stream down her face. She attempted to run but her legs wouldn't move. It was as if they had been weighed down with the weight of all her troubles. For whatever reason he had the Captain yanked her necklace off her neck then dropped it on the ground before stepping on it. Rotten John then picked her up and carried her onto the Siren's Chanty.

    "Ready the ship to sail!" The Captain yelled.
Erika's hope disintegrated, her friends didn't have time to rescue her. She hoped they found Victoria before the Captain found them. If only she had remembered the Captain telling them he would find them once they had the feather.

11 IDA

Ida rushed toward the southern pier while Peter sluggishly ambled behind her, "Come on Peter, we must hurry." She walked quickly through the streets, her mind only focused on finding the Greed's Venture. At last the pier came into view. She scanned the ships hoping to see Victoria's ship. The ship in fact, wasn't difficult to spot due to the fact that it was the only ship docked at the pier.

The Greed's Venture was the most plain, worn down ship Ida had ever seen. She had expected it to be magnificent but was instead, disappointed.

She looked to Peter who looked equally crestfallen, "Is this really the right ship?"

He shrugged, "I don't know, I've never seen the Greed's Venture before."

They walked over to the ship and started to climb the rope ladder that lead to the deck of the ship. Once aboard, they found Victoria sternly ordering her crew around. From behind her, Ida cleared her throat. Her aunt turned around.

"Ida, Peter, I'm so glad you've made it. I've been worried sick that the Captain had gotten you. Where are Erika and Taria?"

"We had to split up to find this ship. They should be at the eastern and western piers." Said Ida.

Victoria nodded, "I will send some of my crew to go and retrieve them." She turned around, "Virgil, Silas, Simon, go and find Erika and Taria at the other piers and bring them back here." She then turned back to face Ida and Peter.

"Now, tell me all about the ball."

Ida's face lit up as she rehearsed the night of the ball. She told her aunt what color of dress she had worn, who she had danced with, and how beautiful the music was. She finished her retelling as Victoria's crew arrived with Taria.

"Where's Erika." Asked Ida. A crewman, the one Victoria called Simon, held something in his hand.

"I'm sorry miss; this was all we could find." He dropped the object he held in Ida's hand then walked away.

Ida stared down at the object in horror as tears began to form. Erika's locket lay broken in her hands. The metal locket was bent and no longer closed correctly. The picture of her grandparents was gone. Victoria tried to comfort her by patting her arm.

"We'll find her… I promise." Without warning gunfire rang out. Ida felt a flare of pain in her right shoulder and was thrown back a bit. She touched the area and when she pulled her hand away it came back red with blood. In shock she turned to Victoria beside her. Cries of alarm sounded across the ship. She put a hand on Victoria's shoulder as crewmen shouted, "It's the Siren's Chanty!"

Her aunt looked at her in comprehension then noticed the blood seeping out of her shoulder where the bullet had hit her. Ida collapsed and was caught by Victoria who called for Peter and Taria once laying her on the ground gently. On the ground Ida fought to keep conscious as her friends attempted to stop the bleeding. The world kept fading in and out of focus as she lost a lot of blood.

Ida heard Victoria ask Peter where the feather was. Teeth clenched Ida answered, "Erika has it." Taria pressed harder on the handkerchief they were using to staunch the blood and Ida let out a hiss of pain.

An arrow with a small piece of paper on it hit the ground a few inches away from Ida's face. Victoria ripped the paper off the arrow and read the message on it aloud.

"It has come to my attention that you are withholding traitors among your crew. Return them and I will see that they get what they deserve. If you do not do what I have asked of you the little Princess will pay with her life. And I assure you it will be a slow and painful death. Meet me at Devil's Gate in one week's time. In all sincerity, Captain William Hilyard."

Ida's only hope was that she would be alive and well enough to rescue Erika. Ida's shoulder refused to stop bleeding and Victoria ordered one of her crewmen to find a doctor then threw him a bag of coins to pay whoever was willing to help.

Ida began to fall unconscious. She heard distant voices say, "Ida stay with me. Stay awake." The voices slowly faded away and she closed her eyes as she drifted into unconsciousness.

A long while after this Ida awoke in a dimly lit bedchamber. Victoria sat in a chair next to the bed she laid in.

"Ida, how do you feel? Are you alright."

Ida groaned, "I feel as if I have died and come back to life."

Victoria laughed nervously, "We thought you had died. After you fell unconscious a doctor finally arrived. He said the bullet had pierced an artery in your shoulder. He took the bullet out but it was nearly impossible to stop the bleeding by the time it did stop you were so pale it was hard to tell if you were alive. We traveled to Avaria as fast as we could in a day. While on the ship we took turns watching you. When we reached the island you had been asleep for so long we were worried you wouldn't make it." Victoria's voice cracked.

Ida tried to shift positions but quickly stopped when pain shot through her shoulder, which was now in a sling.

"How long have I been asleep?" Victoria swallowed nervously.

"Three days."

Ida stared at the ceiling as she thought. She only had four more days until the confrontation with the Captain. She started to get out of the bed. Victoria scolded her and lectured her about how she wasn't supposed to walk yet. Ida refused to do as she was told and stood anyways. Her body weak from blood loss was barely able to hold her up. Instantly her knees buckled and Victoria grabbed her just in time. Her aunt placed her back in bed despite her rapid protests.

"Please let me go somewhere besides this room. Anywhere

else would be better than sitting here staring at the wall."

"No. You will not leave your bed... at least not today. Now I have to leave for a moment. Do you promise to stay in your bed?"

Ida waited a minute to answer and her scowl deepened, "Fine. I promise to stay in bed."

Satisfied, Victoria left leaving Ida alone. Ida began to position herself so she was sitting on the side of the bed with her feet on the cold stone floor. Victoria had made her promise to not stand or walk but hadn't said anything about sitting.

She rubbed the soft cotton of the nightdress she wore between her fingers as she thought about Erika being captured. She knew her sister would be courageous; she had always been the brave one in the family. A cool draft ran through the room despite the fire in the fireplace on the side of the room.
Ida shivered and added another pillow to the one beside her then slipped her legs back under the covers. She tried to gently lift her injured arm from her side. Fire blazed in her shoulder and she made a noise like a cat's hiss. She clenched her teeth together and dropped her arm limply to her side.

The door opened and Victoria, Peter, and Taria entered the room. Ida quickly pulled the bedsheets up a little higher with her good arm when she saw them. Peter appeared unusually nervous as he handed her a single red peony.

"I hope you are feeling much better after your ordeal."

Ida smiled and shyly took the flower with her good arm, "Considering I am no longer bleeding to death, I would say I am recovering just fine."

Everyone but Victoria chuckled at her poor attempt at a joke. Her aunt sat in the corner reading while Peter and Taria told her stories to keep her mind off of Erika. But before long Ida became tired and Victoria forced her friends to leave.

That night Ida slept fitfully and with nightmares. She dreamed that she stood on a cliff that overlooked choppy ocean waves. Across from her the Captain held Erika close to him. A long jewel encrusted dagger lay only an inch away from her heart. She began to run toward her sister but it was too late. The Captain plunged the dagger into Erika's heart.

Ida awoke to Victoria stroking her hair to calm her. Her

aunt whispered reassuring things to her as she sobbed into her shoulder.

  The next day, determined to leave her room, Ida dressed herself as quietly and carefully as she could, which took quite a while due to her arm in a sling. She then went to find herself some breakfast while trying to look healthier than she felt.
Since she had not left her room since she awoke it only took her a few minutes to become hopelessly lost in the maze of white marble corridors. As she walked she repeated in her head only three more days, three more days. Up ahead a door opened and a girl with brown shoulder length hair entered the corridor.

  In her arms the girl carried a basket full of linens. The girl's face brightened and she curtsied when she saw Ida.

  "Good morning your highness, I'm Katherine, is there anything I can do for you?" The girl sounded slightly French.

  "Um, yes, would you be so kind as to point me in the direction of some breakfast?" Ida said quietly.

  The girl nodded, "Of course m'lady, if you would just follow me." The girl, Katherine, led Ida down the hallway a little farther and to a large oak door, "This would be the dining room miss. Are you in need of anything else?"

  Ida smiled, "No thank you."

  The girl curtsied again then turned and walked back the way they had come. Before Ida even opened the door a shout echoed throughout the hall.

  "Ida... Ida where are you?" She knew it was Victoria looking for her. She opened the door and entered the room before her aunt could find her.

  Two men sat eating their breakfast at a table in the middle of the room. At the sound of the door opening and closing they turned to look at Ida. Instantly they stood and bowed.

  "Your majesty, it is a pleasure to make your acquaintance." Said the man on the left in a French accent as Ida was almost blinded by his snowy white hair and beard, "I am Antoine Bataille, and this is my son Caleb." He motioned to the young man next to him, "I also have a daughter who works in the castle named Katherine."

  Ida thought of the servant girl who had just helped her, "I believe I just met her just a moment ago."

Antoine smiled goodheartedly, "Come, you must eat." He motioned towards the table. Ida gladly joined them and ate until Victoria found her at last.

"There you are." Her aunt said relieved, "I was beginning to think you had gotten lost." Ida was just about to tell her she was fine when Victoria cut her off, "What were you thinking? You know perfectly well you should not be out of bed. If it was my choice you wouldn't even be moving a muscle in that bed."

Ida stood, "I truly am sorry Victoria, but I just couldn't stay in that bed doing nothing while Erika is being held captive by the Captain."

Her aunt sighed, "Please tell me next time you decide to go gallivanting off to who knows where."

Ida smiled, "I will."

Antoine and Caleb stood up, "M'lady." Said Antoine as he bowed to Victoria.

"Antoine I see you have returned from your journey safely, it seems you are doing well Caleb." Replied Victoria with a smile and nod of her head. She once again spoke to Ida, "It seems… since you are clearly feeling better it is time for your training to begin."

Puzzled Ida said, "Training for what?"

Victoria smiled excitedly, "Your training to become Queen of course."

12 ERIKA

Blindfolded, Erika struggled as Rotten John threw her in the brig of the Siren's Chanty. "You can't do this!" She yelled as he pulled the blindfold off her then locked the cell door with a gold key.

He smiled but didn't laugh at the scene she presented. "I think you'll find I can." He hung the key on a hook across from her cell then left the room silently.

Erika surveyed her home for the time being. Straw had been pushed into a pile in the corner to act as a bed. There were no windows which most likely meant she was in the belly of the ship.

She faced the key and attempted to put her arm through the bars and grab the key to free herself. Her hand and arm began to slide through bars but became stuck when she was only an inch away from the key. She pulled her arm back inside the cell. She needed a little extra arm length to reach the key. Looking around the cell she decided her only hope was to find some straw strong enough to hold the metal key.

She dropped to her knees and slowly began to test each piece of straw's strength. She tried many pieces until finally one of them was strong enough.

She reached her arm through the bars once more with the piece of straw in hand. She slowly maneuvered the piece of straw through the ring the key was hooked onto. She began to carefully lift the key off the peg it hung on. As she began to slowly bring the key closer to herself the ship rocked knocking the key off the piece

Stolen Heirs of Avaria

of straw. Luckily Erika caught it before it could reach the ground. She then put the key into the keyhole and turned it until the lock made a soft click and the cell door swung open.

"Thank goodness." She muttered to herself. She slowly walked to the door Rotten John had gone through and opened it just enough she could see into a hallway. The only other door in the hallway was closed. She walked up to the door and put her ear against it. Through the door Erika heard two men speaking.

"You will do as I say or your amour will not live to see the next dawn. Am I clear?" Resigned the second voice said, "If I must I will do it, but only for her."

The second voice sounded like the Captain. But who was the Captain speaking to? Who was <u>Her</u>? Was the man talking to the Captain blackmailing him?

Confused Erika hurried back to her cell in the brig where it was safer for her to be at the moment. She locked the cell and returned the key to where it had been before. As the night or what she presumed was night passed on Erika couldn't fall asleep. All she could think about was the conversation she had overheard.

Sometime later Rotten John awoke Erika from her few hours of sleep and gave her a meager meal of moldy bread and foul water. She picked the edible little bits out of the bread and ate them but refused the water that looked as if algae were growing out of it. As she ate Rotten John stood across from her cell waiting.

"What is the Captain going to do with me?" She said.

Rotten John picked the plate and cup up as she finished eating. He turned to leave but before he did so he threw her the keys to her cell then said, "The room across the hallway."

Erika was silent as he left the room. Was Rotten John helping her? If so, why would he? She came to the conclusion only entering the room across the hall would answer her questions.

She opened her cell then walked out of the room and into the hallway. She opened the door across from the brig to reveal a dimly lit room. Erika entered the room suspicious of the circumstances.

"I'm glad you understood my instructions." Said a deep quiet voice. Erika turned to see Rotten John comfortably sitting behind a desk. The Captain's desk, the same desk that housed the map to the last legendary weapons Excalibur and the hammer of

Thor. "Sit down please." Said Rotten John as he motioned to a wooden chair in front of the desk.

Erika hesitantly walked to the chair and sat down. The wood beneath her groaned under her weight. "What are we doing here?"

Rotten John put a finger to his lips to silence her, "Do not speak so loudly or we shall be caught."

Erika was now perplexed. Why would they be caught? Wasn't Rotten John working for the Captain? "Caught by whom?" Erika asked in a small voice.

"We shall be caught by Him."

Did he mean the Captain? Or maybe he meant the man the Captain had been speaking to before.

"Why are we here in this room?" She tried again.

Rotten John pulled an old yellowing paper out of the desk and laid it out on the desk. It was the map. "You and your sister have found the phoenix feather. For which we are grateful. We could never have accomplished the task without you."

Erika hung her head in shame; it was only because of her that the Captain now had the feather.

Rotten John continued, "Now we ask you to find the next item. Mjolnir, the hammer of Thor."

Erika studied the map, "Why would I help you or the Captain?"

Rotten John looked at her sadly, "Not all people are who they seem to be. At one point in life everyone will wear a mask to hide their real self from the world."

Erika tried to wrap her head around this. Was Rotten John talking about the Captain? She was about to ask him what he meant but was cut off.

"I will only reveal the location of the hammer if you agree to tell no one of our arrangements."

The room was overrun by silence as Erika fought with herself internally. She needed the location of the hammer but was the cost of working with the Captain worth it? Impulsively she said, "I'll do it." She couldn't go back now.

Rotten John smiled showing his rotting teeth, "Excellent." He pointed to a place on the map, "This is where Mjolnir is. I believe you have heard of the island nation of Avaria." Said Rotten

John.

Erika nodded, of course she had heard of it. Supposedly she was a Princess of the nation.

"Well." Said Rotten John, "The hammer lies in a cavern below the island. To be exact it is directly beneath the castle."

"Once in the castle, where should one go to find this cavern?"

Rotten John pulled out a roughly drawn map of a building she realized must be the castle. He put his finger in the middle of the oldest part of the structure, "This is the throne room. From here you must go through these corridors to get to the oldest part of the castle." He traced the many hallways and Erika tried to memorize the complicated path. "Once you get to the oldest part of the castle you must find the door with a large scorch mark on it. Only that door can get you to the cavern."

"What is past the door?" Asked Erika.

Rotten John shook his head regretfully, "I don't know what awaits you there. But you will be tested and when you don't know which way to turn… choose the right, and you will get to where you need to be."

She nodded as Rotten John stood up.

"Now, you better return to your cell. I do not know what will happen to you next but remember, everyone wears a mask."

Erika stood then slowly walked to the door. She looked back as she left the room. What would happen to her? The second in command on the ship did not even know what the Captain would do to her. She walked back to her cell and lay down on the straw. What time of day was it? How long had she been on the ship? Questions ran through her head as she stayed in her cell for what felt like forever. No one came to get her. She almost thought that the Captain had forgotten about her when the door finally opened. Erika quickly stood as the Captain came into the room with some rope in his hand. He unlocked her cell door that she had locked again after her talk with Rotten John.

"Turn around and put your hands behind your back."

She obeyed and the Captain tied her hands together tightly. He then led her out of the brig and down the hallway, and then through the room she had talked with Rotten John. They then went through another door in the room and up some stairs to find themselves on the deck of the ship.

Erika greedily took in her new surroundings. The ship was docked at a small rocky island with a small path that led to the top of a small cliff.

The Captain yanked on her arm and she was forced to exit the ship. The Captain pulled her up the path that led to the cliff. When they finally made it to the end of the path Erika saw what she thought was a figment of her imagination. She saw Ida. Her sister seemed the same to her except one of her arms was in a sling.

The Captain stopped a few feet away from her sister. He held onto Erika by her tied up hands, he unsheathed his dagger and angled it a few inches above her throat. Understanding dawned on Erika and she realized what the Captain was planning to do. He was going to kill her. Tears formed and silently slid down her face. I don't want to die, thought Erika.

"Please." Said Ida, "I'll do anything you want just please don't kill my sister." Erika quivered slightly as the cold knife touched the skin on her throat. A line of warm blood appeared and dropped down her neck.

Behind Ida, Peter and Victoria ran to the scene unfolding above the sea and the Captain's gaze turned to Victoria.

"I have to, I have to do it or he'll be angry." He began to crazily shout about the person called He.

"William." Pleaded Victoria, "Please do not do this. I know you are a good man. You mustn't do this."

The knife drew away from Erika's throat and drops of water landed on her face. The Captain released her and began to retreat back down the path they had come. Only then did Erika realize the Captain was crying.

"I am sorry my love." He whispered as he passed Victoria.

Ida ran to Erika and gave her a one armed hug. Victoria watched the Captain leave as a single tear slid down her face.

"We cannot let this happen again." Said Victoria, "Ida must become Queen in order to protect Avaria and all who live on the island."

13 ERIKA

A choir sang like angels as the doors to the throne room opened. Everyone stood as Ida, dressed in a gown the color silver, which was one of Avaria's national colors, slowly walked down the aisle. Silence hung in the air so thick you could cut it with a knife. Ida got to the end of the aisle and kneeled on a pillow before the Archbishop. Everyone sat back down.

"Do you Ida Fillmore, solemnly promise to govern the people of Avaria according to the respective customs and laws?"

"I do."

"Will you in your reign practice justice in all your judgements?"

"I will."

The Archbishop took her hand and led her to the throne. He draped the crimson robes of state over her shoulders then she sat down on the throne. The Archbishop then took the crown from a pedestal and reverently placed it upon Ida's head. He turned towards the audience and announced, "Your new Queen."

The room erupted into shouts of joy that turned into a harmonious cry of, "Long live Queen Ida." Ida smiled as she forgot all of her troubles.

All of a sudden the door opened silencing the crowd. The Captain strode into the room with his crewmen not far behind.

"Sorry to interrupt the celebration."

Chaos broke out among the guests as the Captain walked up the aisle. Ida drew the hidden knife from under her bodice and everyone quieted down.

"What are you doing here?" She said boldly.

The Captain threw back his head and began to laugh, "It seems I didn't receive an invitation." He said ignoring her question.

Victoria slowly approached the Captain, "Please leave William. There is nothing for you here."

Ida saw the pained expression that momentarily flashed upon the Captain's face.

"I'm here because I want to be here."

Ida knew he must be lying, "Why do you want to be here?"

The Captain unsheathed his cutlass, "It's about time you've learned the truth."

Victoria came to stand by Ida. Her hands gripped an axe she had retrieved tightly, "Drop your weapon."

The Captain obeyed and his cutlass fell to the floor with a clang.

"Now tell us what you claim is the truth."

The Captain stepped forward and Ida aimed her knife at his heart.

"Truthfully," He began, "I wish none of you harm." He looked pointedly at Victoria with raw emotion in his eyes. "I am forced to work under the influence of a man who wishes to rule Avaria as king."

Ida looked around at all the guests present. How could anyone believe such false nonsense? "You lie!"

"No." Said someone from among the crowd. Erika, who had been silent throughout the exchange, stood. Not able to meet Ida's eyes Erika said, "He speaks the truth."

"How do you know that?" Asked Ida.

"When I was taken captive on his ship I overheard him talking to a man. The man threatened to kill his amour... his love, if he did not do what was commanded of him. Then, when he had the chance to kill me, he didn't and disobeyed orders putting the woman he loved in danger." Erika looked up to Victoria as she said the last sentence.

Ida motioned to the guards waiting for orders behind her, "Take this man and his crew to the dungeons for the time being."

The Captain held something up in the air, "Wait. Here is the map to find the last two weapons, Mjolnir and Excalibur. And here is the feather of the phoenix"

Ida took the map and feather from his hand, "This changes nothing."

The Captain nodded then willingly went with the guards with his crew following suit.

Erika slipped from the room as shouts of surprise began to be made from the guests as the feather healed Ida's shoulder. She knew what she had to do now. She had to find Mjolnir, the legendary hammer of Thor. She remembered where it was, she remembered the map. She only hoped nobody would miss her as she dashed down the corridor toward the oldest part of the castle. By the time she made it to the door that would lead her to the hammer she was sure someone was searching for her.

She opened the old scorched door that screeched once moved. Dust rained down on her as she looked at the staircase that gradually disappeared. She gathered what courage she had and entered the stairway.

Erika ran down the winding staircase that seemed to go on endlessly. By the time she had gotten to the bottom she was breathing hard. When she could breathe normally she began to walk down a hallway that was entirely made of marble and lit by golden candelabras. The hallway came to a point where it branched off into two different directions.

Erika sat down against the cold wall, downhearted. She didn't know which way to go and was losing what precious time she had left. She tried to remember if Rotten John had said anything about which way to turn. As she searched her mind for an answer she remembered what he had said.

"When you don't know which way to turn... choose the right, and you will get to where you need to be."

Maybe Rotten John had been literally telling her to go on the path to the right. She stood and hesitantly turned to her right and continued on. Down the hallway the candelabras slowly turned into burning torches and the marble to gray stone. She stared ahead as the torches disappeared and she entered a small cavern.

In the middle of the space was an ancient man with a long white beard. Erika thought about how strange it was for him to be there. His clothes were even stranger; he wore an amber tunic that fell to his knees, white linen trousers, and a navy blue cloak. In his hand he held an ornate staff. Yes, definitely strange.

She vaguely recalled Rotten John telling her that she would be tested but she did not know what the tests would be.

The man lifted his hand as if beckoning her to stand directly in front of him. She walked towards him with askance. Once in front of him he said in a strong voice that didn't match his appearance, "Are you a seeker of the hammer of Thor."

Erika nodded, "Yes, I am."

The man disappeared then reappeared ten feet away behind a pedestal, startling Erika. He opened a book that had appeared with him, "The hammer of Thor can only be obtained by completing three tests. Your first test begins now."

Erika blinked and her surroundings changed. She now stood in the middle of a meadow in front of a table filled with all manner of weaponry. What was she supposed to do?

"This is your first test." The man's voice echoed around her but did not come from a certain direction, "You may pick one weapon."

Erika chose the bow and quiver of arrows from the table and slung them over her shoulder, "What am I to do with the weapon?"

"That depends on you."

From behind her she heard a familiar voice, "Hello little Princess." She turned around and came face to face with none other than the Captain with his cutlass in hand. She gripped her bow tightly in her left hand and slowly took an arrow out of the quiver with her right. She didn't know what was happening. How was the Captain here?

The Captain made a sound like a growling animal, "I should have killed you when I had the chance." Erika rubbed her neck where the cut had recently scabbed over. "In fact, I think your friends and remaining family would love to see you dead." He taunted her even as she held his death in her hands. Why was he acting this way?

The Captain charged at her with a cry of anger. Surprised Erika stumbled backwards. She quickly raised her bow and let the arrow fly. The Captain fell to the ground. Blood stained the wildflowers and its metallic smell wafted through the air. Breathing hard Erika stepped backwards until she touched the

Stolen Heirs of Avaria

table.

The voice sounded again, "You have proved yourself to be courageous in your actions. You have passed the first test."

Once again in the blink of an eye Erika's surroundings changed and the bow and quiver of arrows disappeared. She now found herself in a forest.

The voice spoke again, "Welcome to the second test."

Erika looked around her; nothing seemed out of the ordinary. As she turned around to better view the area a dirt path materialized in front of her and she began to follow it. She ducked under tree branches and hopped over large rocks as the path went deeper into the forest. When she began to worry about completing the test she came to a village in the heart of a clearing.

She went into the village but became confused as she discovered it was abandoned. She looked through all of the houses but no people could be found. Then she met two little girls by a well.

"Hello." She said to them.

They turned towards her and one of the girls said, "Who are you?"

"Um, I'm Erika Fillmore." Erika looked around the town once more, "Where are your parents?"

The girls smiled at each other gleefully, "They're in the mountain with the dragon."

Erika furrowed her brow, "What do mean they are in the mountain with the dragon?"

The girls laughed, "They're in the mountain with the dragon."

Frustrated Erika tried to calmly say, "And where is this mountain with the dragon?"

The little girls pointed a finger towards a small hill with scorch marks carved into it.

"That is the mountain."

Erika turned away from the girls to stare at the hill, "Is the dragon on the other side of the hill?" She asked. When there was no answer she turned to see that the little girls had disappeared. She turned around again to see that the village had also disappeared into thin air. It was as if it had never been there in the first place.

She sighed in annoyance as she started towards the hill, "It better be this way." She muttered to herself. As she walked the hill grew closer and the closer it became the larger it appeared. As she approached the hill Erika realized the hill wasn't what it seemed to be. The hill wasn't a hill at all. The hill was the dragon.

Erika gasped as she saw the giant mound moving up and down, breathing deeply. She then sighed in relief, the dragon was asleep. Now she had at least a little chance of finding the villagers. She walked around the dragon to see dozens of people in a large cage. By the cage was a table and on the table was Mjolnir in the center of a pile of gold.

Erika didn't know what to do. Did she rescue the villagers or did she take the hammer? Beside her the dragon shifted almost rolling onto the cage of people. She had no time. She had to rescue the people before the dragon killed them.

The people noticed her as she was a few feet away from their cage. From the looks of it they had been locked up for far too long and had had nothing to eat since then. The people began to whisper to one another excitedly.

Erika pulled a pin out of her hair and started to pick the lock on the cage. The dragon shifted again and Erika found herself staring into a green snake-like eye of the beast. The dragon was awake. Erika hurriedly twisted the pin and the lock unlocked as the dragon roared in anger.

With the people able to get out of their cage Erika grabbed Mjolnir from the table leaving the gold untouched. Electricity surged within her. The power of the hammer was now hers to control.

She walked up to the dragon, hammer held high above her head. As the dragon prepared to attack she threw Mjolnir as hard as she could into the belly of the beast. The sky rumbled as the hammer struck its target. The end result was so bright Erika had to look away. A boom sounded so loudly her ears began to bleed. When the light dissipated the dragon was gone having been disintegrated. Mjolnir was left in the middle of a gigantic scorch mark.

As the villagers disappeared Erika carefully stepped across the smoking ground. She slowly bent down and took hold of the hammer. As she touched the handle her surroundings changed once more. She found herself back in the cavern she had started in. The old man once again stood before her.

"Erika Fillmore, you have passed the three tests. You have proven yourself courageous by not being dissuaded from your task even when placed in danger. You have proven yourself compassionate in your dealings by choosing to help others. And you have proven that there is no greed in your heart. You may take Mjolnir and leave. But beware; those who will want to take the hammer away from you will do so by any means necessary."

Erika nodded then turned back towards the way she had come, hammer in hand. She ran through the hallway and up the staircase as fast as she could. She hurried to show the hammer to Ida but became lost. She did however find the throne room and set Mjolnir on Ida's throne. She then once again went to find Ida. She was wandering down an unknown hallway when a hand clasped over her mouth and another bound her hands together. Erika struggled against her captor but didn't succeed in escaping. "Stop struggling." Said a man in an accent that sounded slightly French, her captor. A bag was thrown over her head and she was led somewhere she did not know.

14 IDA

Ida could not find Erika, it seemed as if her sister had disappeared after the coronation ceremony which had been hours ago. She raced through the gardens, "Erika." She yelled. At this very moment Peter and Victoria were searching the castle and Taria was searching the village nearby, "Erika." Ida yelled once more.

A muffled scream that came from behind her caught her attention. She quickly whirled around towards the sound. There she found Antoine holding Erika a few yards away from her. Antoine must've been the man threatening the Captain. Ida's eyes grew wide as he raised his sword. She tried to run to her sister's aid in what short amount of time she had left.

"Goodbye Princess." Said Antoine as he swung his sword down and impaled Erika from behind. Erika gasped in pain and surprise. Antoine let go of her and she collapsed on the ground. Antoine then gave Ida a sinister smile before running to the beach where a boat was waiting to take him to his ship.

Ida ran to her sister's side, "Erika, please don't die. Don't leave me."

Erika looked up at the sky as blood began to fill her lungs and dribble out her mouth, "Now I'll get to see mother and father, Will and Thomas, grandmother, and everyone else we have lost in this life."

Ida sobbed as Erika lay dying before her eyes. She would have done anything to save her sister.

Erika looked up at Ida for the last time, "Ida… promise me you will never give up and beat the man who did this to me. Don't let my death weigh you down. Live your life and become the great Queen I know you will be someday." With the last of her strength Erika smiled, closed her eyes, then grew still.

Ida's heart broke, the only person she had left that she had not wanted to lose, she had lost. As she carefully took the broken locket out of the pocket of her dress and returned it to Erika. She whispered to herself, "I promise."

She stood and turned to where Antoine had begun to sail away and took a few steps toward the beach. Antoine caught her eye and grinned wickedly, then turned back towards his crew and began to shout commands.

Ida heard someone come up behind her and turned to see Victoria drop to her knees beside her dead niece.

"Who did this?" Asked Victoria.

"Antoine."

"How could he betray me like this? I was so blind I didn't see his treachery. I could have prevented this from happening."

They all could have prevented Erika's death, but failed in doing so. They had all been deceived from the beginning.
Ida stared into the distance; it seemed inconceivable that Erika was truly gone. She couldn't bear to look at her sister's body; it would make everything seem too real. Tears streamed down her face as she began to walk back to the castle. As she passed Victoria she said, "Start the preparations for the burial."

As the week went by Erika was buried by her grandparents in the royal cemetery of Avaria. During that week Mjolnir was found on Ida's throne and was given to the Queen for safekeeping. Ida kept to her room looking at the map and trying to find where Excalibur could be since everything on the map was far too light to be read. She sent Victoria, Peter, the Captain-who had been pardoned of his crimes-and Taria to go and try to find Antoine.

After a while Ida began to become restless as she stayed in her room alone. When she couldn't take being in her room any longer she moved to the gardens and spent her days there. She had no one to keep her company since most everyone was searching for Antoine. So she sat alone day after day until they finally came back.

The castle gate opened and Ida looked up from the flowers she had been staring at. Victoria and Peter were back along with everyone else. She looked them over as they made their way towards her. Victoria had a split lip, a cut along her cheek, and blood staining her dress. Peter looked worse, the skin around his eye had become an ugly shade of purple, he had a split lip, his nose was slightly askew, and his hair was matted in blood.

Victoria excused herself to go see to her injured crewmen, leaving the two alone. Out of nervous habit Ida started to run her fingers through a piece of her hair, "What happened?"

"We were ambushed by a part of Antoine's fleet of ships."

Ida became hopeful, "Did you see Antoine?"

"No."

Ida's hope diminished.

Peter looked her in the eyes, "Are you okay?"

She nodded but unshed tears gave her true feelings away. She tried to hurry and wipe them away but the dam had already broken. She knew he had meant how she was doing after Erika's death.

Peter moved towards her and she found herself wrapped in his arms. They stayed like that for a good ten minutes while Ida cried into his shoulder. Peter stroked her hair, "Ida, I have to go. I need to help the crewmen that were injured."

She looked up and pushed him away, "Please don't leave me again." She couldn't bear to lose anyone else close to her again, "I can't lose anyone else."

His face showed different emotions. After a moment he finally said, "I'll never leave you to defend yourself alone. But I must go to help care for the injured."

Ida watched him leave as she whispered, "I'm sorry." She then went back to the castle and made her way to her room. Upon entering her quarters she quietly locked the door behind her. She rang the bell that alerted the servants of her needing something. She waited until the servant door opened to reveal Katherine crying.

"Oh miss I'm so sorry. I had no idea my father would do such an evil thing. Please don't fire me or my brother Caleb. We had nothing to do with our father's plan and have nowhere to go."

Ida held a finger to her lips to tell Katherine to be quiet,

"Katherine, I know you had nothing to do with anything your father has done. If you were in league with him I would be dead already." Katherine's crying stopped, "But I do need your help. I need a way to sneak out of the castle unseen and acquire a ship that can take me where I want to go."

Katherine smiled through the last of her tears, "I can help you with both of those things. There's a secret passage in this room that leads you to the beach on the far side of the island. I also happen to know someone who owns a ship. His name's Heinrich. He's a merchant that just so happens to be docked on the island for now. I'll tell him to meet you at the end of the passage."

Ida smiled in gratitude, "Thank you. Now where is the passage?"

Katherine walked over to the wall and pulled a tapestry down to reveal a small wooden door, "Here it is."

"Thank you for helping me Katherine. You are free to go now but please don't tell anyone about this."

"Of course m'lady. I won't tell a soul." Katherine then left Ida alone.

Ida grabbed a small bag and put a few of her gowns that she had had from being aboard the Captain's and Victoria's ships just in case the voyage was very long. She then slipped a black cloak out of her wardrobe and clasped it around her neck and pulled the hood low over her face. She took one more look of the map to make sure she would be going in the right direction then slung her bag over her shoulder and set off through the passage.

The passage was dimly lit and the stone floor became dirt as she traveled farther and farther. Katherine hadn't told her how long the passage would be but Ida imagined it was fairly long to connect the far side of the island to the castle. She began to walk faster. Someone was bound to find her missing sooner or later. The tunnel ended and opened up to the sky slowly becoming a deep orange. She kept going forward and saw the beach through the trees. As she became nearer the crash of ocean waves became louder. A man was waiting for her on the beach beside a small boat.

"Are you Heinrich?" Said Ida.

The man rubbed his thick black mustache, "Yes. Come aboard and I will row us to my ship the Smoldering Dragon."

Ida did as he said and stepped into the boat gingerly while holding up her skirts. Heinrich pushed the boat into the water and then jumped in and began to row them to the ship in the distance. They reached the ship and as Ida boarded it every activity came to a stop as the crew saw her and all bowed before her.

She blushed in embarrassment, "Um... don't let me keep you all from your work." One by one they went back to what they had been doing.

Heinrich boarded the ship behind her, "Queen Ida, come, let me show you where you will be staying. Then you can tell me where we are going." Heinrich led her to a cabin just off of the main deck, "I hope it is to your liking."

Ida put her bag on the small bed in the corner, "It's perfect."

Heinrich smiled, "Now come, dinner is waiting."

Ida followed him once more to a dining room below deck. On the table sat two plates of roast pheasant and goblets of water. Heinrich pulled a chair out for Ida, she sat then he sat at her left hand side. They began to eat.

"Now my Queen, pray tell where we are going."

Ida put the goblet of water she had been drinking from down, "Are you familiar with the tale of Atlantis?"

He scoffed, "Of course I'm familiar with it."

Ida smiled, "And are you also with the island Avalon?"

He froze in thought, "No m'lady."

"Well, one version of the legend goes that King Arthur was mortally wounded at the battle of Camlann. His sister, Morgan Le Fay, and the lady of the lake took him to the island of Avalon. Morgan Le Fay hid King Arthur's sword, Excalibur, deep inside the island after her brother's death."

Heinrich stared at her confused, "But the stories of Atlantis and Avalon aren't real; that's why they're legends."

"Really Heinrich, you live on an island that the rest of the world doesn't even know exists. I believe that Atlantis and Avalon are one and the same."

Across from her Heinrich choked on his roast pheasant, "You mean to say that this place is real?"

"Yes. And that is where you are going to take me."

"But why... what is so important about this island?"

"I need Excalibur and Avalon is where it lies." Ida picked up her goblet again.

"But where is this island?"

Ida pulled out the map she had put in the pocket of her dress and laid on the table, "I believe it is here." She pointed to a spot of ocean west of Avaria and South of Ireland. She stood making her chair fall backwards. Then rolled the map up and handed it to Heinrich.

Heinrich struggled to stand as his chair caught on the table, "The journey shall be moderately short. You should rest your majesty. We should arrive at our destination by tomorrow morning."

Ida nodded to him and turned to leave the room. Heinrich practically ran to open the door for her and bowed lopsidedly as she left to go to her small room. As she walked to her cabin the crewmen stared at her curiously. Behind her, Heinrich scrambled up the stairs and began to shout orders to the men on deck.

Once inside the walls of her room, Ida pulled her boots and cloak off and climbed into the bed fully dressed. She lay down on her back and stared into the black space above her as she then drifted to sleep.

The next morning Ida quickly changed then clasped her cloak around her neck before joining the men on the main deck. Heinrich manned the helm.

"Good morning your highness. We should most likely be arriving on the island soon."

Ida glared at the sea ahead of her, "What do you mean by most likely?"

Heinrich swallowed visibly, "Well, the map was faded and hard to read so I'm mostly guessing where we should be going." He glanced at her sideways looking nervous.

"Oye Captain." Said a man from the crow's nest.

Ida and Heinrich looked up at him.

"I see land."

Excitement built up in Ida as she looked ahead to a small rocky island in the distance. As they traveled closer to the island the men began to prepare to make port in front of a cave entrance. Ida smiled joyfully as she realized that she now had a chance to find Excalibur before Antoine.

Ida looked closer at the cave. Above the opening carved into the stone read, The Maze of Morgan Le Fay. Her heart pounded in anticipation, she had found the way to Excalibur.

15 IDA

As the ship laid anchor Heinrich gave Ida a torch and some flint and steel to light it. Her first try she lit the torch and put the flint and steel into the pocket of her dress. The crewmen lowered the gangplank and she walked onto the rocky soil with fervor.

Once off the ship Ida started towards the open mouth of the mountain with her torch in hand. Water dripped from the cave's opening creating a small waterfall. She motioned back at Heinrich and his men to follow her then unsheathed her knife with her free hand.

She began to walk slowly through the darkness unsure of what was to come. The only sounds that came through the darkness were the echo of water dripping from the space above her and the sound of the footsteps of Heinrich's crew. Up ahead, a pinpoint of light began to grow bigger and brighter the deeper into the cave they went.

Finally, they entered a large brightly lit cavern with a dark passageway opposite of her. A sign on the wall read, those who enter the maze of Morgan Le Fay shall either be rewarded, or pay a terrible price.

Behind her Heinrich said, "M'lady, are we really going to enter the maze? The sign does say we may have a terrible price inflicted upon us if we do."

Determined Ida said, "You may go back if you wish, this isn't your quest."

She started forward into the maze not waiting to see what

the crewmen decided. She felt a hand on her shoulder and turned around to see Heinrich smiling at her, "I would never forgive myself if this was the last time anyone ever saw you."

Ida nodded and they set out down the dark tunnel. The air became colder the further along they went. More than a couple of times the group came to dead ends and had to turn around. Ida became frustrated. They had to be getting close to the end, they just had to.

All of a sudden one of the crewmen screamed loudly and pointed at the wall. Everyone stared at the man who seemed to be frozen in fear.

"What is it?" Asked a man that stood next to him. The question was left unanswered as another scream echoed through the darkness. One by one the men succumbed to their fear of whatever they saw on the walls.

Suddenly Ida knew what the men were seeing, or at least what she saw was similar to what the men saw. Water cascaded down the wall creating a glass-like effect. She stared at it and the images of her dead family stared back at her. Tears formed in her eyes as she looked at her parents, her brothers, Erika, and her grandmother.

She wanted to stay there with her family forever but reluctantly turned to glance down the tunnel. Should she keep going? It all seemed pointless in the end. Antoine had most likely already found Excalibur anyways.

What was she thinking? Antoine had no idea where the sword was. She realized the cave was messing with her mind. She tore her gaze from the image and looked around her at Heinrich and his crew. They all seemed to be staring at the wall while water continued to flow over it. She took a step towards Heinrich and her foot splashed into a puddle of water that seemed to be growing. Slowly realizing the gravity of the situation, Ida shook Heinrich by the shoulders. He groaned and put his face in his hands while muttering, "My Lucy, my poor, poor Lucy."

The water grew higher until it was almost to Ida's knees. She shook Heinrich again more frantically, "Heinrich it's not real. The cave is just trying to keep us occupied while it kills us." Heinrich looked up at her, "We need to move on now." Heinrich nodded and the pair began to try to awaken the crew members from their magic induced state.

Half of the men awoke from their stupor but the others refused to come with them and were left to drown. As the group moved on through the water now hip height Ida cried for the men they had left. From behind her she heard Heinrich whimper every now and then as the water reached shoulder height and they were forced to half walk half swim. Ida held the torch above her head but a spray of water hit it and the fire went out leaving them in the pitch black terrified. The water continued to become higher until they were swimming through the passage.

In the front Ida swam with her knife in front of her disoriented of which was she was going until she hit something solid in front of her. Heinrich crashed into her creating a ripple effect among the crewmen. Ida felt along the solid thing that she presumed was a door. Her hand came to a handle and she opened the door releasing her and the men into a lit chamber of polished marble.

Heinrich jumped up and hurried and closed the door which was still releasing water into the chamber. Ida stood and walked around the chamber that was an odd circular shape. Along the gleaming walls were doors all the same shape and made out of the same material. In the middle of the chamber was a stone with something sticking out of it. Ida saw that it was a sword in the stone. On the rock a plaque read, here lays the sword in the stone. The one who is kind of heart and valiant in all their actions may retrieve the sword and become the master of fate. On the hilt of the sword was the name of the weapon.

"Excalibur." Whispered Ida to herself.

All of a sudden a door on the far side of the chamber opened and Ida gasped in shock. Peter, Taria, and Victoria all tumbled into the chamber soaking wet. The three of them closed the door together then turned around and stared at Ida in horror.

"Ida?" Said Peter, "What are you doing here?"

Ida frowned, "It seems I could ask you the very same question. What are you doing here?"

Victoria interrupted their exchange, "If you don't mind, we came here for the same purpose. Now are we going to get what we came here for or just stand here?"

Ida and Peter glared at one another as Victoria tried to pull the sword out of the stone. No matter how hard she pulled however, the sword would not budge.

"Let me try." Said Peter as he stepped towards the stone. He tried but couldn't pull it out either. Next Taria tried and then Heinrich and all of his remaining crew.

After everyone but Ida had tried and failed Ida said, "Could I try?"

Peter groaned in frustration, "If you can pull it out it would be a miracle."

Ida gave her torch to Heinrich then turned towards the stone and closed her hand around the hilt of the sword. In her hand the sword grew warm to the touch and as she pulled the sword slid out of the stone like butter. Amazed she held the sword up as everyone gasped in surprise.

"How?" Asked Taria.

"The sign on the stone. It says that whoever is kind of heart and valiant in all their actions may retrieve the sword." Ida looked to Victoria, "Now how do we get out of here?"

Victoria looked around the chamber, "I believe one of these doors should get us safely back to our ships."

They all nodded in agreement as Victoria opened the door she was next to. The doorway was sealed with what seemed to be big gnarled tree roots. Ida crossed the room and opened a door that also revealed tree roots. Everyone began to open all the doors and all but one was closed off by tree roots. The one door that didn't have tree roots opened to a tunnel brightly lit by torches in sconces along the wall.

Ida entered the tunnel and everyone else followed her. The new tunnel didn't hold any hidden dangers as the tunnel before had, it simply sloped up as the group moved on. They finally made it back to the main cavern where all the torches in the room were blown out by a cold draft circling through the room.

Ida searched her pockets for the flint and steel Heinrich had given her. After feeling nothing but fabric she found the small cool pieces of rock. She pulled the rocks out of her pocket and struck them together over the torch she had given Heinrich. Slowly the sparks caught the edge of the canvas on the torch once again and began to cast shadows along the walls.

The group began to move along the tunnel towards the

ships, but before they could exit the cavern another dimly lit light grew brighter in the same tunnel they were just about to go through. Footsteps echoed through the same tunnel. The light became bright enough to cast shadows on the walls of the cavern and the holder of the torch came into view.

"William. I thought I had made it clear you were to stay on the ship." Said Victoria grimly.

Equally as grim the Captain said, "I would have stayed on the ship if it hadn't been a week since you first came into this blasted place."

"What do you mean?" Said Victoria, "We haven't even been down here for a full day."

Magic must make time flow differently down here thought Ida.

"We need to get back to Avaria now." Said Ida.

Everyone as fast as they could scrambled through the tunnel towards the ships. This time Ida traveled back to the island with her aunt and Heinrich gave his word that he would never speak of their expedition to anyone. Sailing back to Avaria was unusually uneventful and they quickly made it back to the island.

What they came back to was exceedingly different from what they had left. Chaos now reigned on the island. Ida got off the ship and ran to the village as fast as she could. Almost all of the buildings had been burned down. Her companions came running behind her. Stunned they all stood there for a few minutes.

"How did this happen?" Ida asked.

Victoria turned away from the village and the others followed suit, "Antoine has arrived to claim the island much sooner than we have expected."

All of them ran towards the castle where men were lined up ready to fight. Caleb and Katherine came to greet them as they came closer to the castle, "We were hoping you would be back soon." Said Caleb as he sheathed his sword.

"What has happened in our absence?" Asked Ida.

Katherine wrung her apron in her hands, "It's our father. He has come to claim the throne. He and his army are camped on the far side of the island and are preparing for war.

16 IDA

Ida knew this day would come, "Caleb, I need you to go to the village and find all of the survivors and bring them to the castle." He nodded and began to run the way they had just come. Ida looked to Katherine, "I need you to help all of the injured villagers." Katherine ran back to the castle. Ida turned back to her companions, "We can use the stables behind the castle as a base. I'll find the feather and Mjolnir then meet you there as quick as I can. Prepare the army for war."

Before anyone could say anything Ida turned and fled into the castle. She ran through the corridors until she came to her own room. She flung the door open and found the weapons. She then changed as fast as she could into the clothes the Captain had given her. Without wasting any time she ran to the stables where her companions were waiting for her and set the weapons against the wall.

Then, the war began and Ida's and Antoine's armies began to exchange crossfire.

In the stables Ida looked at a map of the island as Victoria, Peter, Taria, and the Captain looked at her gravely. Antoine's forces outnumbered Ida's three to one. There was only one way to win the war. Ida turned her gaze to the feather, sword, and hammer laying against the wall to her right.

"We must use them." Said Ida as she went to collect them in her arms.

"It really is our only hope of victory." Said Victoria.

Ida handed the feather to Taria, "You must go and heal our wounded soldiers on and off of the battlefield."

Taria nodded then left.

Ida then gave Mjolnir to Peter and kept Excalibur in hand, "The rest of us will fight until our final breath."

Victoria put a hand on her shoulder, "If we die. We die in honor."

Together they exited the stables and walked towards the battle. Throughout the once beautiful field, soldiers and blood were scattered across the vast space. The soldiers that were still fighting were beginning to lose hope and were becoming weary.

The four of them joined the battle. Ida looked for Antoine in the midst of the throng of soldiers. A man came to challenge her but she slashed her sword across his middle and he fell to the ground. One by one every soldier that fought her joined the fallen until no soldier was brave enough to challenge her. She spotted Antoine fighting Victoria across the field.

Ida then did what she had been longing to do ever since she had pulled the sword out of the stone; she looked into Excalibur's blade. At first nothing happened, and then slowly, terrible images began to appear. The sword showed Antoine and Victoria dueling. Ida stared wide eyed as Antoine knocked her aunt to the ground then raised his sword ready to strike like a snake. He swung downwards right into Victoria's middle. The Captain then appeared onto the scene. The sword showed Antoine knock the Captain to the ground then again raising his sword and striking his target.

Ida looked up from the sword to Antoine who was still fighting her aunt. She ran as fast as she could determined to not be late to save a life again. She watched helplessly as Antoine knocked Victoria down and struck the final blow.

"No." She screamed. She had to get there before the Captain was killed too. She was almost there. The Captain joined the fray and again Antoine raised his sword, and then swung downwards to his intended victim.

All of Ida's emotions turned to rage. She wanted revenge. Her run slowed to a walk as she neared the murderer.

"Antoine! This ends now. I challenge you to a duel."

Everyone that heard the challenge issued stopped fighting

to stare at her. A duel was a very serious matter on Avaria. The loser of a dual didn't just face embarrassment or a mere beating; if the loser wasn't dead already the punishment for losing was death.

Antoine paled then began to smile like he knew a secret no one else did, "I accept. You can choose the weapon. Your highness." He said the last sentence in mockery towards her.

Ida nodded, turned, and then started toward the stables. She knew what weapon she would choose. She grimaced at the thought of dueling on the field already draped in sweat and blood. The custom on Avaria was for the duel to take place in the exact place it was challenged at dusk the same day. She sensed someone start to walk beside her.

"What have you done?" Said Peter as he took hold of her arms stopping her in her tracks rather abruptly. As he faced her Ida stared past him careful to not look directly in his eyes.

"You know exactly what I have done." Ida tried to wiggle out of his grasp but he kept an iron grip on her, "I had to do it. It was the only way."

Peter sighed, "It was the only way to do what? Save the kingdom and end the war, or get revenge."

Ida stopped struggling, "Both. I feel the need to protect my people and avenge my family's deaths. This is the only way I can try to do both. This war shall end with blood, and it will either be mine or Antoine's."

Peter let go of her, "If I can't stop you at least let me help you."

Ida glared at him, "Fine, you may help me. But if you hinder me in any way." Her hand tightened around Excalibur.

Peter frowned as he saw her hand on her sword, "I promise you I will do everything in my power to help you win the duel. I just don't want to see you fail."

Her hand dropped from the hilt of her sword, "Good. Now come help me find some armor and sharpen my sword." She held Excalibur up so he could see the dried blood that coated it.

When they were only a few yards away from the stables Peter hurried to get to the door first. He held the door open for her and she marched right in without glancing his way. She walked to the table in between the horses stalls then sat on a bale of hay and began to clean the blood off of her sword.

Peter hesitantly sat across from her. They sat in silence. As she cleaned Ida thought about all her dead relatives. Would they be proud of her? If they were still alive would they say she was doing the right thing? Or would they persuade her to back out of the duel? Sunset wasn't even an hour away. She could back out right now. No… she wouldn't. If Antoine didn't die thousands of other people would. She had to stop the bloodshed.

She looked to Peter, "Will you go find a sword for Antoine to use and some armor for me?"

With a nod of his head he left, and slipped away to the armory. Ida really was alone now. She didn't even know if she had Peter to rely on. She scrubbed her sword even though it was already clear of all blood. Sunset was in a few minutes. Would she really have a fair chance to win the duel? Could she kill Antoine if she had to?

Peter came back into the stable with two swords in hand but no armor. With a worried look he said, "Your army is using all of the armor at the moment so I couldn't find any for you. We don't have time to go searching for some. Sunset approaches, we should best be going."

Ida nodded and led the way into the crisp air. A crowd had already gathered around the spot Ida and Antoine would duel. Antoine was there as well, "Decided to show up now did you."

Ida ignored his taunting as Taria entered the ring to tell them the rules, "No biting, spitting, or any other foolishness that could be called cheating." She looked pointedly at Antoine when she said this, "The loser of the duel shall be executed." She looked to Ida, "The weapons."

Peter handed a sword to Antoine and Ida unsheathed Excalibur. Antoine's face grew red, "She must fight with a regular sword. It is against the rules of the duel to fight with that." He pointed to Excalibur.

Taria looked at Ida fearfully, "He is right. You cannot use that sword." Peter traded swords with Ida, "Now…" Taria paused for a moment, "The duel shall begin."

The opponents circled one another as they looked for each other's weaknesses. Then the action began. Ida slashed at Antoine's left side and he easily blocked the blow. She twirled around and struck his arm leaving a large gash that began to bleed.

He roared in anguish then struck her sword with a powerful blow. Ida's sword clattered to the ground. She dodged Antoine's next two strikes. The cries around them grew louder each second Ida came closer to death. She needed her sword. Antoine swung his sword wildly and she rolled to safety and retrieved her sword. The odds were once again balanced between the two. As they fought on Antoine seemed to grow weaker. Ida could tell he was tiring. His movements became sluggish as the sky turned from orange to indigo. At last Ida found the moment she had been waiting for. Antoine let his guard down and she slashed at his legs causing him to crash to the ground. The people around them went silent. Antoine scrambled to stand but gave up when Ida kicked his sword away and laid the tip of her sword against his chest right above his heart.

"This is for my family." She said so quietly only Antoine could hear her.

He looked her in the eyes with his penetrating gaze, "I hope it was worth it."

Ida swung her sword over her head. This time he would be the prey, and she the predator. She never looked at Antoine's lifeless body as she turned towards the battle field and began to walk away from her crowd of spectators. At last she could stop worrying and fully live her life. She was relieved and a little angry, but felt sadness most heavily. She was sad that her family had been taken away from her because of the selfish desires of one man. Instead of meditating on her thoughts she decided to examine the battle.

The ending of the battle was grave. Rain clouds had gathered over the island and began to turn the churned up grass into mud. Ida stared across the field. Across the bodies of friends and foes alike, the figures of two people in particular caught her attention. Victoria and the Captain lay side by side, they had held each other's hands for the last few moments of their lives; and that is where they had died. At last, at peace with one another.

Tears streamed down Ida's face; she really was without family or guidance now. She wiped at her face then turned back towards the castle. If she was truly alone, she would learn how to become stronger and live day by day how Erika had lived her short life, bravely.

Peter and Taria came to stand next to her holding the feather, Mjolnir, and Excalibur.

"We need to hide these weapons." Said Ida.

"Where?"

Ida shifted her weight from foot to foot, "I know just the place where they will never be found."

Peter put a hand on her shoulder gently, "Where?" Ida started to walk back towards the castle with Peter and Taria by her side, "The bottom of the sea."

ABOUT THE AUTHOR

Michelle is a lover of fine books. She can often be found reading in her snuggie or watching old musicals. Her love of words inspire her to create her own stories which fuels her reading passions. Michelle lives in a small rural town in central Utah.